A Little Christmas Music

Stories of the Season

A Little Christmas Music

Stories of the Season

by C.W. Gusewelle

Illustrations by Lon Eric Craven

 KANSAS CITY STAR BOOKS

A Little Christmas Music, Stories of the Season
Published by Kansas City Star Books
1729 Grand Blvd., Kansas City, Missouri 64108

First edition

Library of Congress Card Number: 2006931953
ISBN-10: 1-933466-22-7
ISBN-13: 978-1-933466-22-4

Project Coordinator: Doug Weaver
Illustrations: Lon Eric Craven
Design: Jean Dodd
Printed in the United States of America
  by Walsworth Publishing Inc.
  Marceline, Missouri

In memory of William Bleifuss,
teacher and friend

Table of Contents

The Luck of Small Places

She was a great international beauty who had starred in movies and on the stage, and who, if you could believe the magazines, had shared the tents, so to speak, of important generals, a famous Italian tenor, two cabinet ministers and a Saudi prince.

That tent-sharing business wouldn't win a lot of points with folks here in Deer Crossing, population 1,210. But she was a beauty all right, even if she did show a little wear. And when she stepped out of her stretch limo in front of McGee's Farm and Home — a vision in white fur coat, fur hat and fur boots — Miss Purity Devore just about stopped traffic on the courthouse square.

Argus Mooner, the half-bright stock boy, was coming out of McGee's with a fifty-pound sack of horse feed balanced on each shoulder, headed for a customer's pickup truck, and when he saw the lady I thought he might go to his knees right there.

People on foot stopped and turned. A man starting out of town in his car took a hard left instead and made a second pass around the courthouse for a better look. Across the street, you could see faces pressed to the windows of Buck Campbell's law office and the Burger Joy.

The limo driver was squatted down, staring forlornly at the puddle spreading on the pavement underneath.

"I'd guess it's your water pump," I told him.

"You think that's it?"

"I'd say so. That or a hose. It's too far back to be the radiator."

Miss Devore turned to me with those famous baby-blue eyes under painted brows.

"Are you a mechanic?" she demanded to know.

"No, ma'am. That's just a guess about the pump."

"What are you, then?"

"I'm the newspaper editor," I told her.

"The *what*? You mean this place has a newspaper?" She was incredulous.

"It's a weekly," I said. "The office is right across the street there, upstairs over the bank."

"I suppose you'll want an interview," Miss Devore said, making a face about it.

"No, ma'am," I told her. "We don't go in for that. We mostly run high school football scores and items from our country correspondents. Family reunions and hog roasts and such."

She seemed surprised, maybe even a little bit disappointed.

"Well then," she said. "Maybe you could tell me where I'd find a lounge."

"A ladies' room, you mean?"

"No, not that. Just someplace a person can sit and be comfortable and have a little refreshment."

"Oh, a saloon! Why didn't you say so? There's two," I told her. "Bud's Stagger Inn is around the corner and down half a block. It's the cleanest, and they have a pool table."

"You're sweet," she said, and headed off in the direction of Bud's, high heels clicking, fur coat swinging. And maybe she wasn't queen of the world, but she was sure the queen of this small place where bad luck had stranded her at half past 1 o'clock of the afternoon before Christmas.

Ralph Morganer's garage was only three doors off the square, so the driver climbed back in and some of the others of us rolled him into the shop by push-power. Ralph didn't have his head under the hood more than 10 seconds.

"It's your water pump all right," he said. "She's shot."

The limo driver groaned.

"Good thing you stopped when you did, too. Otherwise you'd of burnt up the engine."

"Can you get me running?"

"*Haw!*" Ralph snorted. "Ford truck? No problem. Chevy? You bet. But that thing? Pump'll have to come from the dealer, in Dallas, or maybe Oklahoma City."

"How long?"

Ralph looked at his watch.

"If they was to get it out yet today, which I doubt, and nothin' runnin' tomorrow, and everthing jammed up with the holidays and all — I'd say maybe next Tuesday if we was lucky, or Wednesday pretty sure."

"*Wednesday?*" The driver's voice came out a squeak.

"That's to *get* the pump. Then it'll take a couple hours to put it in, an' you'll be rollin' again."

"Wednesday's too long," the driver said. He was a nervous little man in a uniform that needed pressing. "We have to be in Chicago day after tomorrow. She's got a show there that night."

"Who does?" Ralph had missed the spectacle out on the street.

"The lady I work for," said the driver. "She's an entertainer."

"Maybe you could get a plane in," I said. "We've got a little strip outside town."

"What do you think a plane would cost?" said the driver.

"Don't know. I never hired one. But seeing as she's a star —"

"She is," the driver said. "And she was a real big one, too. But in show business people forget. Things are a little tight right now."

He turned back to the mechanic.

"Well, I'd say you're stuck." Ralph wiped his hands on a towel.

"Couldn't you patch it in some way just to get us by? You know, *improvise?*"

"Listen," Ralph said, "I wouldn't mind improvisin' on a chain saw or a ridin' mower or something like that. But when you're talkin' about a vehicle that costs maybe forty grand —"

"Sixty, actually. New, that is. Anyway, the car's rented."

"Forty or sixty — whatever. You don't mess around with some jack-leg patch job. You get the right part."

"I'd be responsible," the driver said.

"Don't matter."

"I'll put it in writing. Just try, please."

"I don't know . . ."

*   *   *   *

The rest of us kind of drifted away and left them to settle it. I climbed the outside wooden steps to the office of the *Clarion Advertiser* on the second story over the bank, where Marge was pasting up some pages.

Friday's our publication date, and of course tomorrow's Christmas issue was out early. But with the holiday, she was working ahead for next week. The way we see it at the *Advertiser*, news doesn't have to be new to be good.

"Bud Baker was just in," Marge announced. "Said he has a big problem over to the saloon."

"What sort of problem?"

"Something about that woman. He said if I saw you I was to tell you to come over there right away."

"Why me?"

"Because he heard you sent her."

I really didn't much care to mix in it, but Bud was a good advertiser, half-page a week. So I had to go.

"Call him," I said. "Tell him to meet me out front of his place."

Bud was waiting on the walk, looking pretty worked up.

"What's the deal?" I asked him. "Is she misbehavin' or what?"

"It's not her," he replied. "She's just sittin' there drinkin' her sody water."

"Well then?"

"It's the men," Bud said. "Look around you. There's not a man on the street."

He was right. It was a fine, bright day — wonderful for the season, with only a cool little breeze stirring the courthouse flag. But men were missing from the picture.

"It's pretty quiet, all right."

"That's because they're all *in there!*" he said. "A crowd like you never seen. Everything in town that wears pants. Even the preacher."

"That ought to be good for business," I said.

"Business, nothin'! It's the second-biggest day of the year, and I haven't done a nickel's worth in the last hour. They see she orders a sody water. So some of them gets a sody water, too. The rest stands around, pretendin' to talk. But every one of em's eyin' her kind of sidelong."

"She's something to see," I told Bud.

"That's not the point of it," he said. "She's killin' me. You got to give me a break here."

I told Bud I'd do what I could. Then I went back around to the newspaper office and called my wife.

"We've got a situation," I told her.

"It's with that woman, I expect."

Word travels fast in a town like ours.

"Is it true," said my wife, "that you're her main adviser?"

"Don't be silly," I said. "Their car broke down, and I tried to help out, that's all."

"I know that." She was laughing. "So what's the deal?"

"First thing, we got to get her out of Bud Baker's saloon. Then we have to find a place to put her up. They're going to be stuck here at least overnight. Maybe until sometime next week."

"There's the motel."

"I just called there. They've only got eight rooms, and with all the people back for Christmas they're full up through Sunday. Ralph Morganer's got a sleeping loft up over his garage. He said the driver could stay there."

"It's just the lady then? Well, bring her here, for Pete's sake. We've got room."

I was fairly sure that's how it would turn out. My wife's always been a big one for taking in strays. After all, she took me in.

"We can put her in Amy's room." Amy's our daughter — 14 years old, but trying hard to be ten years older. "And Amy won't mind sleeping on the couch."

So that's how it worked out.

I drove over to Ralph's shop, to get Miss Devore's things out of the trunk of the limo. Ralph had the pump out, and was breaking it down on his bench. Then I picked up the lady at the Stagger Inn. Bud Baker wrung my hand like I'd saved his life, and I thought he might weep for happiness as I led the lady out. In the rear-view mirror, I could see a great gang of men — grinning like apes, their eyes still shining — standing on the walk outside the door of the saloon as I drove away.

"It's a sweet little town you've got here," Miss Devore said. "Nice people."

"Most of them are," I told her. "It's like anywhere."

"But what do folks do for night life?"

"Not too much. There's TV, and high school ball."

"Wow," said Miss Devore. "Wow."

"Then of course there's special occasions, like tonight. Christmas eve, every year, we have a party. It's a town tradition — about as long as there's been a town, I guess. It's in the gym, with a stage at one end. The school dance band plays, and there's skits and whatnot. And a Santa for the little ones."

"I'd like to see that," she said.

"Sure. Everybody comes. The kids have been decorating all afternoon.

After I drop you at the house I've got to go over and help set up tables and chairs. You'll stay in our daughter's room."

"She won't mind?"

"It's usual, when we have company."

"What's your daughter's name?"

"Amy. Really it's Amity, but she likes Amy better. She's 14. And, you know, at her age everything's an issue."

Miss Purity Devore looked out the side window at the bare trees and the clapboard houses of Deer Crossing as they went by. It was several moments before she spoke again.

"Yes, I almost remember," she said finally. "I was 14 myself once. It was a long time ago."

*   *   *   *

It was nearly six when I got back from the gym. Betty Sue and Amy were talking at the kitchen table.

"Seems like Amy's got a new friend," my wife said.

"Is that so?"

"They chattered away in there for most of two hours."

"Well, she's *nice*," Amy said, kind of defensively. "And she's not — I mean she's not at all like you'd think."

"What do we think?" I asked.

"You know. Snobby and fancy and stuck up. Things like that. But she's not. She's just like anybody, and she's easy to talk to."

"So what did she talk about?"

"For one thing, she likes my room. She likes it a lot. She said she never had a room of her own when she was a little girl. She always dreamed of having a place like mine, with curtains and pictures and all."

"Really?"

"But she never did. They lived someplace in West Virginia or somewhere, in a trailer. She said her daddy was a coal miner. But he got killed in the mine, and her mother went off with a different man."

"She told you a lot," my wife said.

"Practically everything. An aunt and uncle kept her, but the uncle died. Then she grew up and got in shows and stuff, and mostly now she travels around and sleeps in hotels . . ."

"*And you have my word for it, there's no worse kind of loneliness than that,*" said Miss Purity Devore, who'd listened just for a moment at the kitchen door.

"We didn't mean to talk about you," I said, flustered.

"Why not? It's true. But you know what really got me? It was all Amy's little bottles of nail polish lined up on top of her dresser. Nine different colors. It reminded me how much being 14 can hurt."

As she spoke, I couldn't help noticing the change in her. She'd scrubbed the heavy layers of makeup from her face, and you could see a few more lines. They had a softening effect, though — almost like beauty marks. And the truth is she was prettier than before, although maybe less likely to stop traffic.

"About tonight," she said to Betty Sue. "Can I ask a favor?"

"Depends. What is it?"

"It's about something to wear."

My wife looked at me. "I thought you brought her things."

"He did. But they're my *Look-at-me* clothes, all glitter and fluff. Tonight I'd rather wear something not flashy. Something dark. We're about the same size, you and me."

"Sure, let's go look in my closet," Betty Sue said. "And don't let me forget to make you a name tag."

"Nobody in town really needs one," I told her, "but we wear them just the same. That makes it officially a party."

"Anyway, everybody knows *you*," Amy said.

"That's not so, sweetheart. Hardly anybody does. And don't write my name Purity-anything. Just make it Mattie Boggins, if you will."

"It's a funny name," said Amy.

"I know it. But it's mine, and it's true. And tonight I want to be Mattie Boggins again."

*   *   *   *

Heads turned, as I knew they would, when the four of us walked in the gym.

Nearly all the fellows who'd made fools of themselves at the Stagger Inn that afternoon were there. But the vision in white fur coat and hat and boots was a different kind of vision now. She was a fine-looking woman — in the same way their own wives were fine-looking women, all with some of the same creases of care and experience.

And seeing that, the men lost the sappy-grinning expressions from their faces, and the ladies all relaxed, and the party went forward in the same good spirit as all the years before. The table decorations were handsome and the food was terrific, as you'd expect. In a country place like ours, the art of cookery isn't learned, it's inherited. And the men of the Lions and Owls clubs did a fine job serving, although lions and owls generally make odd bedfellows, so to speak.

After dinner the lights went down. The Dobbinger twins gave a nice program on the cello and flute. The juniors and seniors in the drama class read some Christmas pieces with high emotion. There was a drawing for the door prize — a snow blower donated by Morganer's Auto & Small Engine Repair.

While the drawing was going on, the band carried its instruments in, and it was time for the dancing to start.Some of us men here in Deer Crossing don't dance — never have. I expect we could learn if we had to, but it's just not seen as something we much care to do. Although the young enjoy it, and we don't mind watching.

So that's how the evening went until, on toward midnight, someone had the idea Miss Purity Devore ought to be heard from. The band teacher called her to come up, and at first she didn't want to do it.

"Go ahead," Amy said to her. "I'd really like to hear you."

So, in the end, she did go up. She looked through the stack of music, found a couple of show tunes the band could more or less play, and belted them out in her lustiest Purity Devore manner — that steamy, hard-edged come-hither style everybody knew from the TV and her records. And the people ate it up, believe me. Clapping and whistling and stomping their feet, shouting for more.

She stood there in the soft stage light, in Betty Sue's plain black 10-year-old party dress, and she waited until the racket began to die down. Then waited some more — until you almost thought you could hear the tick of the big clock up on the gym wall, which said 20 minutes until Christmas.

"That was from Purity Devore," she said, her words floating over the silent crowd.

"This one is from Mattie Boggins, who thanks you for bringing her home again."

"*Silent night,*" she sang, "*holy night,*"

"*All is calm, all is bright . . .*"

Ever so softly the boy at the piano took up the old melody, then the girl with the clarinet.

And the voice that filled the gymnasium of the school in our little town that night was altogether different than the voice of just moments before. All the hardness was gone out of it. All the affectation was replaced by the most amazing sweetness.

So that, afterward — long after the season was past and she'd been carried on to larger places and perhaps to further fame — people spoke of it as a moment when they'd heard an angel singing.

A Light Before Daybreak

The worst part, always, was speaking with the parents. No amount of training could prepare a doctor for that. And six years of experience in the hospital's critical care unit had not made it any easier.

The man and woman sprang to their feet as he came into the family waiting area. They were in their 30s, although in their anguish they looked even younger. And they clung fiercely to one another's hands, their faces ashen.

"I'm Doctor Forrest," he told them. "Bob Forrest."

"We saw someone different downstairs," said the man.

"Right. That was in the emergency room. I'm a surgeon. We're evaluating your daughter now," he said.

"Is she conscious?" the mother asked.

She wasn't, the doctor said. Not yet, anyway.

"We'll know more shortly. But she took a serious hit. There's been some head trauma. That much is clear. We're deciding how to proceed."

Even to him, as he spoke them, his own words sounded so rote, so mechanical.

"I was loaded down with packages," the mother said. "I didn't see the car backing, and she just slipped a few steps away."

It had happened in a shopping center parking lot. And in that instant the happiness of the season — and of her world — had shattered like a dropped glass.

That is how lives change, divided in a single moment between all that went before, and all that might follow.

"Julie's nine, and she's strong. Can she . . .?" the mother asked, then faltered. "Will she . . .?"

The young doctor looked into the woman's eyes, which were a dry well, emptied now of tears.

"As quickly as we know something," he said, "I promise I'll be back out to tell you."

* * * *

That had been on a Saturday, the sixth day of December. Surgery had relieved the pressure of bleeding, but the outcome still was uncertain.

For a week the child's mother scarcely left the room. Meals came on a tray from food service, but often they went back almost untouched.

During the days she read aloud from books that were Julie's favorites, even though there was no sign the little girl heard. Nights were spent on a cot beside the hospital bed.

But there was another, younger child at home, who also needed mothering. So the father took time away from work and spelled his wife in the room. Each morning, making rounds, Doctor Forrest stopped at the nursing station, reviewed the charts from the night before, then looked in on the little girl.

"What's the outlook?" the father asked — the same question every day. The same one the mother had asked. And the answer was not much different one day from the next.

"I wish I could say. But with a head injury it's just impossible to be sure," the doctor told him. "Sometimes a coma is part of the healing process. Sometimes it's more than that."

"So the best we can do is hope?"

"I'm afraid so."

The unguarded pain on the father's face caused the doctor to look away, at the girl in the bed.

"She's breathing on her own," he said. "That's a positive sign. And we're keeping her hydrated. It's a matter of waiting now."

"And praying?"

"That, too," said the doctor, although he was trained to put most faith in the things he could control.

Daytimes, Julie never was alone. But as the desperate uncertainty stretched past a week, then two, then to nearly three without visible improvement, there seemed little point in a parent staying nights on the cot in the room.

"Trust us," the nursing supervisor said. "We'll call you, regardless of the time, if there's any change."

*   *   *   *

A hospital at a small hour, when the rest of the world is sleeping, is a strange and still and lonely place.

The reflected glow from the outer hallway made a kind of deep twilight effect in the darkened room, where the child lay perfectly still — as still almost as death — her little chest rising and falling slightly with each breath, caught like an errant moth in a web of tubes and wires.

A row of monitors above the desk at the nursing station displayed heart tracings and other critical information for each patient on corridor 5-East. Routine needs — the taking of pulse and temperature, delivery of medicines, changing bed linens and so forth — were attended to by the night aide, whose name was Sue.

She was a girl from the country, and had dreamed of one day being a nurse, but bad luck and bad choices had been against her. She'd married young, dropped out of school, had borne and lost a baby, then been abandoned by the baby's father.

Those details of her life she kept to herself. She had gone back for her high school diploma, though that was hard, and was studying now to enter nurse training. What the people she worked with knew of her was only that she was pleasant and dependable and had an uncommon gift of nurture.

And she had taken a special interest in the little girl who'd come to them so sadly hurt, her sweet face all but hidden by the bandages that wrapped her head.

Reading the chart, Sue discovered that Julie was 9 — the age her own daughter would have been.

In those silent hours, when her duties had all been done, she often sat beside the bed in that room, and in an unpracticed voice she sometimes hummed a tune of the season, which called back memories of her childhood.

*   *   *   *

Passing by the door, the head nurse stopped and looked in.

"What's that music?" she asked the aide.

"It's carols," Sue said. "I don't sing so good, so I brought in my cassette player."

"I suppose it won't hurt," said the nurse. "Just don't disturb the floor."

"I'll keep it down real soft."

"All right. She may not hear anyway."

"I know," Sue said. "But just in case."

That was just before midnight.

Then the hour hand of the clock moved past the 12, and on into what always, for so very many ages, has been a day of magic.

The head nurse would struggle later to remember just what hour it was. She'd been bent over a notebook, making out the staffing schedule for the weekend ahead, and had looked up, startled, to find the aide standing wordlessly before her.

"I think you'd better come," Sue said.

"What for? *What is it?*"

"She moved."

"What?"

"At least I think she did. Her eyes opened, and I think she moved."

Together they hurried along the hall, and into the room whose twilight was filled with music, and with the words of wonder: *Above thy deep and dreamless sleep, the silent stars go by.*

The child's eyes were truly open.

"I hear it," she said. "And someone was here."

"Who was?"

"I don't know," the little girl said. "But it was someone. Someone so bright."

They called the parents, and gave them the gift of unimaginable joy. And they telephoned Doctor Forrest, who leapt from bed and dressed in a rush.

He hesitated only a moment, to look in with gratitude at his own daughter breathing softly, evenly in her dreams, before he drove the few blocks from home to the hospital.

The nurse and the aide, Sue, told him how suddenly, how unexplainably, it had happened.

Then he stepped with them into the room and took Julie's hand. Quite alert, she looked up at him with clear and perfectly untroubled eyes. In his years of practice, he had never known a patient to come back from the darkness so immediately, so fully restored.

They recounted to him, then, the strange words the little girl had spoken on waking.

Someone was here, she'd said. *Someone so bright.*

And though he was a man finely trained in science and the practical art of medicine, he would be troubled afterward by a new, perplexing uncertainty — never again able to put his whole faith only in what his professors had taught him and what he had learned from books.

The Exile

We suffer very much from the cold. The cold and the stillness, and of course from the separation. With practice, one learns to accept some things. I will not say you ever become used to the cold, but you accept it as a simple fact — like the hardness of the plank bed or the evil smell of an unwashed blanket. Then you do not remember to think of it. So, when I say that we are suffering from cold, my hand writes what my mind knows must be true, Since there must be suffering at more than fifty degrees of frost. But it is a discomfort my body forgets to experience.

With the other, it is different. Stillness and separation you cannot forget. Because the effort to do that, even if unsuccessful, only brings a larger silence, a greater separation.

The house, our prison, is small and poorly made, even for a prison house. The bottom wall is stone, the upper part boards. The single room has a window on each of three sides, a loose-fitted door on one of those, and on the fourth side a hearth for the fire. The planks on which we keep our straw mattresses are at the end nearest the hearth. The walls there are greasy wet, except sometimes in the night when we fail to wake often enough and the fire burns low. Then the wetness turns to ice. On the walls at the other end, the frost comes through the boards — between and through them — and gathers thickly on the inner side like white fur. If we are lucky to catch a hare with our wire, it is not necessary to leave it outside where it might be taken by foxes. We only need to hang it at the far end of the room against the white wall and it remains frozen perfectly hard.

The view from all three windows is quite the same: a plain of snow, stunted cedars scattered singly and in groves across it, and, beyond, at much greater distance, the darker wall of the impenetrable woods. Well, not impenetrable exactly. I have gone into it often, a little way, to set my wire traps. *Endless* is the better word. You could travel through that forest for hundreds of miles, and in one direction a thousand miles or more, without meeting another living soul unless by the most improbable accident. That is what is fearful about the woods. The walls of this tiny house are not what hold us here. The door is unlocked. We go in and out freely. The hopeless distance from anything is the wall that cannot be crossed.

At the end of summer they come with a boat before the river closes with ice to leave the things we will certainly need. They bring rye flour and a replacement blade for the wood saw, two ax handles, matches, tea, sugar, salt, kerosene for the lantern, some beet roots and usually a large sack of potatoes, which must be eaten quickly before they freeze and spoil.

The rest we must find for ourselves.

Then, again in winter, they come back. When the river freezes they can land a plane on it. For a long time before it arrives, we hear the plane humming in the silence. Then we see it circle in the cold sky, and we put a wet stick in the fire to make smoke so they will know surely we still are alive. Otherwise they might not land. Then the plane disappears behind the trees. And pretty soon there is the sharper, thinner sound of a different motor, and they come out of the far woods, two of them riding on a snow machine.

We wait. The machine stops. They open the door of the house, and look at us. "You are alive," they say, seeming surprised and actually pleased.

"You see us."

"You're the tough ones. In Number 24 they are all dead."

They always speak of places in numbers. We can't know where 24 is, or who is — or was — there. We have no map.

"Dead isn't so bad," I tell them. "There are worse things."

"Don't complain. Anyway, we didn't put you here. You put yourselves. Do you have tea?" There has been time enough from first hearing the hum of the plane until they arrived at the door to melt snow and boil the pot.

"Do you have chocolate?"

"Greedy rascal!" One of them takes the two bars from the pocket of his coat. "Yes, I have chocolate."

"Then we have tea. And is there mail?"

"None. There was a letter for Number 24, but no one there able to read it." There never is any mail. Probably it is even a lie about the dead men receiving a letter.

They do not stay long — a half-hour at most. They do not even bother to remove their hats and fur boots in the cold of the house. They empty the woodbox and look in our sacks and under the straw mattresses.

They are supposed to be looking for weapons, but they are half-hearted about it, only going through the motions, knowing that we have nothing except what was brought to us. And what is a weapon? You could kill a man with a saw or an ax, if it came to that. They finish their tea. And, saying, "Keep alive, then — a little longer," they go out to pull the rope to start their machine, whose racket carries them across the white plain until they disappear, a single dark moving speck, into the larger darkness of the forest.

For several days, until the next snow, the track left by the machine remains and is almost companionable. Then, in a night, it vanishes. After that there are only the occasional, brief marks of my own snowshoes crossing the emptiness to check the wires in the edge of the woods. That's how it is when they come in winter, as they will do again soon. Between times, nothing. Everything here is flat — the land, the light, time itself. All perfect flatness.

*   *   *   *

Petrov is rotten company. To anyone who lives in the usual way, among people, it would mean nothing. So what if some fellow were a tiresome fanatic? So what if every discussion led, sooner or later, into some mysterious nonsense? What difference would that make? Leave him, then! Go out, away! Find someone else more interesting to speak with.

But not here. There is nowhere to go out to. Petrov is, of all things, a Baptist — one of, I think, about seven in the whole country. Possibly fewer. The Frenchman, Sartre, wrote that Hell is the others, and he was right. The incredible and absolutely brilliant maliciousness was to put us here together. Petrov condemned for his illegal proselytizing. Me for having written a tract which I intended only as harmless pornography, but which happened to offend an official who imagined he saw his girlfriend in my story. Now Petrov is my Hell, and probably I am his. Two years we have been together, with still eight more to go, on the chance we last that long. So, as a character in that Frenchman's play said, "Let's get on with it."

It was his turn to get up last night and put on more wood. He forgot, or was absorbed in his prayers. Anyway, he didn't do it, and I woke this morning to find the fire a cold, gray ash and the white fur of frost beginning to form on my stinking blanket. I screamed at him, swore at him. He lay, pretending to sleep, until my curses all vanished into the longer silence. Then, when the new fire I had lighted began to warm the place a little, he got up without a reply of any kind and went immediately to work on the thing he was making.

"What goes on in that head of yours?" I asked him.

He just bent over his block of wood, shavings curling from his knife.

"Answer me, Petrov," I told him. "or I'll put you out and bar the door." I could have done it, too. He is half my size.

"I am thinking that whom God greatly loveth, he chastiseth."

"He must love me a lot," I said. "He gave me ten years to spend with you."

Petrov's thin blue lips drew slightly upward in what I guess was intended for a saintly smile.

"And what do you think about?" he asked. Already, for him, it was a month's conversation.

"I have been thinking about when they come next time. Suppose that I ask for chocolate, as I always do. When his hand is in his pocket, suppose I break his head with a stick of firewood. And with that knife of yours you cut the throat of the other one."

"I won't, though. As you perfectly know."

"No, I suppose you wouldn't. So it's no use."

"It's no use," Petrov said.

"All right, then. Let's get on with it."

*   *   *   *

Each day from first light until the lantern is turned out he has worked at his carving. Now that he is finished and has assembled the parts, I can see at last how cleverly it is made. Such alone-ness makes anyone clever.

The walls are grooved, so that they join by just sliding together. Atop those is a shed roof, rafters and other members separately carved. And the figures of the people and the animals are quite delicate and lovely. I am surprised, because I would never have imagined a dull fellow capable of doing that.

"It's not bad," I tell him. "But it needs color."

"I see the colors," Petrov says.

"If you say so." It is unsatisfying even to argue with him. "But be sure to hide it when they come. Or you will land us both in big trouble."

And it is certain they must come any day. I spend time at the window on the side toward the river, looking at the snowfield and the line of woods, watching the sky, listening for the hum of the plane. Thinking of chocolate.

To kill them would be easy. But not for one man alone. It would take two, to do it at the same time. And after that? I still cannot decide what is next. We could take their snow machine, but when its petrol was used up it would stop somewhere in the woods. And where would we be then? Still a thousand miles from anywhere.

"I don't suppose you can fly an airplane?" I ask.

It is blue afternoon, in the low light of the unrisen sun. He is on his knees in front of the table, looking with a sweet, stupid expression at his little carved house. He has lighted a candle in front of it.

"Petrov!"

"I am praying."

"Can you fly a plane?"

His thin blue lips move, but he does not reply immediately. Then he stands up and blows out the candle.

"Forget it," he says. "I won't help you."

"Even to kill them? It would be easy."

"*Especially* that," Petrov says. "I'm no part of it."

"Then we're lost for sure."

"Not necessarily," he says. "I am saved, and maybe you, too."

He always is most contemptibly serene after he has finished praying. The ones who decided to put me in this place with this man knew exactly what they were doing.

The next day, before noon, the faint sound comes humming across the distance ahead of the plane. The black speck appears at the edge of the forest and starts across the white reach of flatness between the scattered cedars. The tea water is warming.

"Where is the can of sugar?" I ask Petrov.

How to explain my excitement? After the empty weeks, the arrival of anyone is a great event. Even jailers are company of a kind. With a little help I would cheerfully murder them, if only I could know what to do afterward. At the same time, I am wonderfully pleased to see them coming — eager for their voices, their chocolate, their bits of accidental news. I can feel my heart pounding with something very like happiness, as I lovingly set out their cups.

The snow machine arrives outside the hut and its racket stops. They open the door and come in, knocking the snow from their fur boots, slapping fur gloves against their padded legs. The great cold has burned white spots on their exposed faces.

"Such frost!" one of them cries. "No one can live in that." Then he looks at us. "But I see you do live."

"We manage to."

"I congratulate you. It's no weather to be dead in."

"Mail?" I ask.

"No mail. You have tea?"

"The chocolate?"

He searches with his hand inside his coat. Then also with his other hand. Both hands are in his pockets at once. The small room seems suddenly very bright, with him luminous in the center of it. I actually can feel the weight of the sharp-edged stick of firewood, although I don't hold it. I only imagine it. Then the instant passes.

He lays the chocolate bars on the table. I am pouring the tea from the pot.

"May I show you something?"

It's the fool, Petrov.

"Something I have made."

The blood leaves my head, and I think I may fall down. I see him go to his bed and reach under the pillow where he keeps his icon, his nativity, disassembled and wrapped in a cloth.

"Look out! What's the matter with you?" one of them cries. I have filled the cup and am still pouring, the tea running off the table and splattering on the floor.

"The — the fire," I say thickly. "I've forgotten the fire."

"What's wrong with the fire? It's good."

"It will go out! I have to get more wood."

"It's fine," they say. But I'm crazy with fright.

"No, you can see! It needs another stick." And I rush out the door.

The air does not even feel cold. The hairs freeze and curl in my nose, and my teeth ache. But there is no other sensation of cold at all. I am flushed hot all over. I can see ten years becoming twenty, or thirty. That does not even require a trial. It can be done administratively.

I would run, but there's no place to run to. So, instead, I go around to the window. The glass is iced in the corners. There is a small clear place in the center of the pane, and through that I can see that he has lighted the candle, and on the table he is putting together his abomination — fitting the cleverly grooved walls, putting the roof atop, arranging the figures of the people and the beasts.

The other two have come close to see. Petrov is on his knees. In the light of the candle his thin lips are moving. In case there was any doubt before, there is none now. He is finishing himself, and finishing me with him. No one ever is guilty alone. Like everything else, guilt is collective.

I think to hide. Luckily it has not stormed for some days, and around the hut we have made a confusion of aimless tracks. Also there are the tracks I have left crossing the immense field to the forest's edge, where my wires are set. Maybe they will believe I have gone that way. Next to the wood pile there is a bush whose branches, weighted with snow, bend against the stack of logs, making a place — a kind of snowy compartment — underneath.

I creep in there from behind, and wait. The flush of anger and fright is gone, and I am shaking now. Will they hunt for me? Maybe not too much. They know how vast the forest is, and no man can get beyond such a wall of distance. So why would they even bother to look? I crouch under the bush, unable to see, and try to imagine the length of an individual minute. They never have stayed very long.

Hinges scrape as the house door opens. Boots squeak in the snow. There is a shout.

It is Petrov crying my name. Followed by a silence. Then Petrov shouting again.

"If you can hear me," he calls. "It is important."

What is important is to remain perfectly still and govern my shaking, so that I do not disturb the bush. Considering the circumstances — the temperature and my vast terror— my control is remarkable.

I hear Petrov cry out a last time. From the sound, his face must be turned away in the direction of the field, which swallows his voice. He calls without conviction. Even with a little sadness. Probably he is afraid to be alone in the trouble he has made. I suppose now he wishes he had agreed to help me kill them. And I would smile at that, except my upper lip is frozen to my teeth.

Then there is the sound of the others coming out.

"We can't wait," one of them says.

"But he has to be somewhere." It's the damnable Petrov.

"The fuel is at Number 24," says the second one. "It's an hour to get there, to take petrol and leave before night. Already it's late."

I hold a long breath, my teeth rattling. Then I hear the pull of the engine rope. On the second pull, the snow machine starts up.

The breath comes out of me in a white cloud. For the first time I can let myself shake. I wait until the sound of the machine is safely away, then I crawl out of that place. The machine is almost to the edge of the far forest. In it, then, and out of sight.

My feet are like pieces of ice as I stumble toward the hut.

"*You see!*" I am screaming at Petrov. "*Fool!*" I am over being frightened. They can't hear me anyway. I barely can hear their distant motor.

"Ruined us both!" I tear open the wooden door. "Ruined," I scream at him. "For nothing." There is something odd in the way my voice completely fills the hut.

"Petrov?"

I hated him, understand. Hated him! But even before the name vanishes in the silence, I am inexplicably, powerfully, lonely for the one to whom it attaches. His carved thing still is on the table. Beside it is a paper, which I light the lantern to read. It is scrawled in haste, but the essential fragments register:

… planned for months … believers, like me … the frontier if we are lucky … would not have left you

… keep the carving, a gift … seek faith … burn this note … stay alive …

There was more, but no need to read it. I stood very quietly beside the table, my head inclined, and listened for the sound of the plane lifting from the frozen river.

*   *   *   *

The cold is worse. There is no one else to help keep the fire in the night.

Sometimes I forget, and when I wake there is hardly a spark left. Then it is almost the middle of day before the white fur goes off the wall.

The cold one learns to forget, though. Because it's a natural thing, cold. The loneliness, the separation, are what's unbearable. I listen at the window, on the chance of a plane. I check my wires at the edge of the wood. And I spend a great deal of time looking at the thing Petrov left — handling it, taking it apart and assembling it again. Moving the figures about.

I am not yet in any way religious. I am just an unlucky sinner, as before. But what he left is the only connection to anything alive. Hands made it. I think of his hands — of his knife making the shavings curl. Of his cleverness. Of the way he called out for me at the last. The figures are almost alive, too. If I burn the candle and look hard at that little scene for a very long time, sometimes it becomes so real that I am drawn into it, and then I get the feeling of being less alone.

I often wonder if they made it in the plane. Eventually, when the ice is out, the boat will have to come again with flour and matches and tea and the rest. Maybe I will ask. I doubt if they did, but, either way, how can anyone know? It's not the kind of news you get here.

One thing I have to admit. I miss Petrov. I miss having him to shout at. The Frenchman was wrong.

A Nativity Story

I t came to pass in the year 2015 that the very last barrel of oil was sucked from the sands of Arabia. A new Surgeon General's Report declared mother's milk a carcinogen. And the Ayatollah Khomeini, vigorous beneficiary of a transplant of all his vital organs, resumed at age 115 his jihad against the Great Satan, the United States.

It was the year, also, when U.S. President Duncan and Soviet First Secretary Marchenko startled their generals by declaring peace. All the missile crewmen came up pale as cave rats out of their silos, and the empty carcasses of the ICBMs were sold off to become lake cottages and *dachas* in the birches.

In that same year, the orbit of the space station Titanic was found to be decaying and plans were hurried forward for a permanent colony on the moon. The population of famished Africa surpassed one billion. And Pope Ruth II amazed the faithful with her encyclical on family planning.

And on one of the last days of the very last month of that two-thousand-fifteenth year of the Christian era, while standing before a mirror in a house in a midlands city whose name, for efficiency, had been reduced to only the zip code 641, it occurred to Hollie Gustavson that she had been alive almost one-fortieth of all the time since people had begun counting the years from the number 1. And although it was true that wonders had been achieved with diet, hormones and, in extreme cases, cosmetic reconstruction, so that in her lifetime age had become largely a numerical abstraction, that did not keep her from thinking of herself as suddenly very old.

The house the Gustavsons lived in, and the ones their friends lived in, looked very much like the houses she remembered from her girlhood in the century before. That is, they stood alone on little plots of ground with gardens of metal bushes and glass flowers, with locks on their doors so that even in the crimeless society perfect strangers could not go freely in and out. Most people were lodged in connected quarters, splendid common buildings for contented common folks, and hardly ever below floor 10. Separate houses were an extravagance of the nostalgic few, built from old plans or recreated from memory and photographs — with porches and swings, widows' walks and gingerbread trim. Sometimes even with detached garages, although with the decline of the automobile they mostly were furnished as guest rooms or gazebos for entertaining.

There were other differences. Windows — or what appeared to be windows — were preserved for tradition's sake. In actual fact they were permanently sealed over to keep the weather out and perfection in.

To anyone passing outside they presented, in daytime, a vision of lace curtains and, at night, of a lamp warmly glowing. but from the inside, by operating the selector buttons, one could cause to be projected in those rectangles at any hour of night or day the scenes of one's own choosing. Would it be amusing to live for a while in a forest? Press a button and the forest would appear, in which titmice flitted from branch to branch and squirrels chattered. If one tired of the forest, mountains would materialize on command. Or a wind-scoured reach of shoreline, with the mutter of waves breaking and the strange, mingled smell of salt and storm wrack and drying seaweed.

When not in use, the windows were mirrors. And it was looking into one of those that Hollie Gustavson saw, looking back at her, the face of a young woman in the perfect bloom of her middle 20s. She vaguely remembered being the age it represented — years ago, before the century turned. *But you can't fool the heart*, she thought. She was a woman of 45 whose children had gone away somewhere in the world. And who, when the year shortened and Christmas came, could recall having once written poetry — but not at all *how* she'd done it, and never exactly why.

"I'm lonesome," she said on the Talk-see to her husband, who'd gone away the week before to 941 on business. "And I don't know how to make the time pass."

"Make it *pass*?" His face on the wall screen registered surprise, amusement. And possibly a flicker of irritation. "Time's not supposed to pass," he said. "The whole point's to stop it."

The man she'd lived with was nearly 50, but unchanged in any important way from the boy he'd been. He had beaten ten thousand cans or more of tennis balls into flaccid submission. He had worn out exercise bikes the way some men wear out shoes. Between them, in the darkness, there sometimes were recognitions. By daylight, he understood her less. But he was a good provider. He had provided her with children, who'd been a temporary joy. And with the house of wonders which might, like him, last practically forever.

"You could put up the tree," he suggested.

"I've done it," she said. "It didn't help." The tree was an appliance, like most all the objects her hands touched. One didn't *put it up*. One called it forth. A lever beside the mantel of the false fireplace was turned. The bookcase of false books spun around to expose the false tree on its back side. The tree's ornamented branches folded down into the display mode and the strands of tiny bulbs winked on. Under the tree were false packages — the "seeds," her children used to call them, from which grew a stack of authentic blessings, although in these last years, with the children gone, the seeds were infertile. All of it was the effortless work of several moments. Turn the lever, and a Christmas was produced entire.

"Have you played the windows?" he asked her. "You know you like Florida." When the windows played Florida, the temperature in the house rose several degrees and hidden fans washed the closed rooms with warm breezes that carried the piping of gulls and the croak of coastal rooks.

"I did that yesterday," she said hopelessly.

"Well, Colorado then. Maybe 805 in the fall. Not the town itself —"

She'd been foolish to think he might understand.

"— but one of the trails. Don't we have the Glacier Gorge tape? I'm sure we do. Play the windows and it will be as good as hiking to Mills Lake in October."

"I'm not in Colorado, though. I'm here in 641 and I'm lonely. It seems like it's been today for a year."

"Play Chicago, then. With crowds of people."

She could sense his impatience. He turned his face sideways to speak to someone else in that distant room. Then, turning back:

"Or Mexico City. Nobody's lonely there. But set the atmospherics in the low range or you'll gag on the fumes."

She was lonelier than before she'd called him.

"Nothing does any good."

"Then take a pill," he said curtly. And the screen went blank.

She wandered through the house, which passively awaited her pleasure. In the family room — a bitter name for what once had been a happy place — her eye fell on the drawer of cassettes. She read the dates on some of them, and for one vulnerable moment she was tempted. At her command, the multiple laser projectors would blink on, and her children would appear there with her in the room. At ages 2 and 6, or 8 and 12, or any age she chose. All the images were stored. Real as flesh, the holographs would move and laugh and speak in the room, quite alive, susceptible to every proof except being touched, shades reassembled out of motes of light but able to burst her heart with love. Then the cassette would end.

Knowing that really shouldn't have troubled her, since her days were composed mainly of illusions. *But some losses don't need repeating,* she thought, and angrily shut the drawer.

Luncheon announced itself in a melodic voice, and the television came on to report the mid-day news. President Duncan and First Secretary Marchenko were shown with their wives, photographing orchids together on a combined vacation in the People's Republic of the Philippines. Disheartend by the ruckus her encyclical had provoked, Pope Ruth had resigned to become the compromise prime minister of the unified Middle East, and the network's satellite cameras were watching for a new puff of smoke from the Vatican chimney. The tray of luncheon food waited under the warming lamp for a measured half-hour before tipping its contents, untouched, into the recycler.

An eternity later it got to be 2 o'clock. What her life lacked, Hollie had decided, was *purpose.* And she had seated herself at her writing table to make a list.

1. Make this list, she wrote first. Then:

2. Don't cry anymore. And after that:

3. Don't play any of the machines.

4. Don't pretend.

5. Try to write a poem. But, finished with illusion, she drew a line through that one, and wrote instead:

5. Read a poem.

6. Make tomorrow's list.

7. Get through the day.

8. Don't call 941.

A voice from the kitchen startled her. It was the call to supper. In the time it had taken to consider the list and write it out, she already had accomplished numbers 1, 2, 3, 4 and 8, and was so near achieving number 7 that she would have to hurry to get to 5 and 6. She could not remember an afternoon flying by so quickly.

That was her first day of Christmas.

On the second day of Christmas, she unplugged the Robo-Chef and fried herself an egg. In real grease. And devoured four Danish pastries.

On the third day, she made and ate a pan of fudge. Then she went to the master computer closet, gathered all the tapes that played the windows, put those in the compacter, and, examining herself in a window-mirror, was pleased to notice that the child-face looking back at her had gotten a hickey.

On the fourth, fifth and sixth days she listened to the frantic buzzing of the Talk-See. And every time her husband's face appeared on the wall screen, peering with irritation at a machine that would not respond, she erupted in a wild cackle. The sound of herself laughing was strange to her. Strange and wonderful.

On the sixth day she unlocked the house and let the doors stand open, hoping strangers would feel free to enter, although as it happened none actually did.

On the seventh day she rested, having remade her own universe.

On the eighth day she actually *did* write a poem. A very small poem, and bad haiku, but a beginning:

With a stranger I
Shared a house without windows
And forgot my name

The next day, the ninth, she got both her children on a split-screen conference call on the Talk-See and read them her poem.

"Are you all right?" they asked her.

"I'm fine," she told them. "In fact, I'm absolutely grand! I look years older already." They invited her to come visit — to stay as long as she liked. And she promised she would when she had gotten her affairs in order.

"How do you look, being older?" they wanted to know.

"Lovely," she told them.

On the tenth day she had a monster sale. People came from all the other marvelous mechanical houses and carried away everything of hers that wasn't attached.

On the eleventh day she packed.

And on the twelfth day of Hollie Gustavson's Christmas — not in daytime, really, but just at dark — she carried her traveling bag out across the plastic grass to the neighborhood heliport, leaving behind a note taped to the door. *To hell with artificial trees,*was all it said. The rest would speak for itself.

Then staring up into the deeps of the real sky, more fabulous than any machine could simulate, she looked for a sign to guide her — a woman of a certain age, and beautiful in the old-fashioned way — believing that whichever star she chose would lead her right.

A Christmas Journal:
Of Travelers and Shepherds
and Men at War

In its simplest elements, the Christmas story

is a story of rescue for men with failing hope,

of strangers meeting and being strangers no more,

of the lost being found, of great beginnings in adversity.

Told across two millenia — and though remembered

now by human beings in diverse circumstances of

comfort and terror — it remains undated. For in it,

in this or any season, those who care to look will

find relevance to their own condition.

They were late coming to the blasted area. Dawn had begun to show over the ragged line of high tropical forest on the far side. They lay in the undergrowth, drawn in close together against all rules, watching ground fog rise and the pale light come in across that place of upflung earth, forbiddingly silent and nitrous-smelling from old explosions.

They lay in the high grass, listening, looking at the sky.

"It's not the right one," Pollard whispered. He was 19 years old. He had taken off his helmet and turned on his side, resting his head on his arm, better to watch the sky and the clearing at once. His whisper rattled through the grass, louder than he'd meant, startling all of them.

"It's the one," said Andrews, ahead and to the left, unseen like the others. "He'll make another pass."

Pollard considered it, full of misgivings. "We're 20 minutes late," he whispered.

"He'll make another pass. They always do."

The fog was gone, now, and the place lay raw and ugly in the brilliance of the young day. They looked the same to Pollard, these clearings. Cratered, made in a concussive instant, they held a presence of violence long after the jungle had forgotten the sound. Lying in the grass with the others, and yet entirely alone, Pollard was less sure than Andrews that they had come to the right place.

The boy's hair was straw colored, nearly white, and plastered wet against the many peelings of his forehead. He examined the earth so near his face. It was dark with the slow-burning humus of untilled centuries, and he was thinking that in some other time he would have liked to put a plow to it, open it to the sun. It would make beans like they had never seen back in Moultrie. But now — now he would gladly trade it for a sterile acre of Georgia red. And, thinking that, he came back again. He lifted his eyes back out across the awful disorder of the rendezvous, and his mouth opened in the voiceless beginning of an alarm.

The deer stepped clear of the foliage then, and out into the blasted area. The boy's mouth closed and he watched as the creature picked its way delicately across the torn clearing. It was smaller than the deer he remembered from his own woods, faintly marked along the flanks, legs delicate as soda straws. As he looked, it was joined by another from the shadow.

They brought peace with them to that place. They seemed to give no notice to the ruin where they passed. Their presence imposed a certain order on what he had come to fear was only incongruity, final and unredeemed.

Pollard turned his face in the grass. "Do you see them?" he would have whispered to the others. But the deer had raised their heads and swung half around toward the far treeline. Frozen against the day, they delivered judgment and were gone in the quick, purposeful bounds of those who mean to survive.

The stillness lay more terrible on the morning. Then an imagined hum became a surer sound behind the trees. The helicopter was on them in a moment, the name *Delta Star* plain on the fuselage, blades cutting a *whop whop* in the heavy air as it began to settle in the dust cloud of its own making. The door was open, with a crewman in it, and somewhere beyond that door — though far beyond, perhaps — was Georgia.

"Now!" cried Andrews in the grass beside him.

And Pollard ran with the others through the waist-high grass and out onto the cratered place where the deer had been.

*   *   *   *

The land slid up out of the gray water, bearing a city on its shoulders, and the white gulls that had been with the ship since morning were joined now by clouds of their fellows, riding the wind on crooked wings and dipping to hunt where the leviathan had passed.

The three young men leaned at the rail, letting the miracle of fingered glass and steel define itself in the haze of the winter noon. On the North Atlantic in that season one learned quickly enough the use of a wool overcoat. The young men's collars were turned up against their ears, which stung fiercely in the salt air. But they would not have stayed inside. For them, this was the beginning of something, and they agreed that it was not good to miss beginnings.

"Have you imagined anything so splendid?" said Livinus.

"Passing belief," said Bocar.

Ten days ago in Southampton, waiting to board a ship, the Africans had met as strangers. Now, in their loneliness for far homes, they were bound in the total intimacy of pilgrims.

Okoro had become their leader. Now, their hearts uneasy, they looked to him for assurance.

Escorted by tugs, the ship seemed scarcely to be moving. The city rose frozen and still above them, with only the gulls to give it life.

"It is very big," Okoro said. "We will see what sort of people are there."

Beyond the bleakness of the pier and the press of the immigration line, Bocar and Livinus stood finally on the windy curb, their suitcases beside them, waiting for Okoro.

"And how much these?" Livinus said.

"The silvers? I believe they are the same as two shillings."

"*Eeeeh!* And I have not even learned *shillings* yet."

Okoro called to them from the door of the customs shed and they went inside with their suitcases again.

"There is no answer," he told them. "The number is changed."

"Changed?" Bocar was alarmed. "Where are we to go then?"

"Who is that one?" Livinus asked. A boy of 5 or 6 years sat on Okoro's suitcase, his red cheeks tear-streaked.

"Our friend here cannot find his parents," Okoro said. "We will take him to the place for lost things. Then we must find a hotel."

They waited in the guard's office while loudspeakers announced a lost boy from Mamaroneck.

"There is no point to cry," Okoro told the child. "See here — does this one cry?"

The boy turned the little carving in his mittened hand. It was a wild pig, cut from hippo ivory.

"No," he said.

"And that one has much to cry about. Many things are chasing it."

"Really?"

The child's parents came in, coats flying. The mother snatched him up.

"He just slipped away from us," the man told the guard. "We've been frantic."

"That man is from Africa," the boy told his mother.

"How nice." She buttoned his coat at the neck.

"He lives in a place where there are real kings and things."

"How nice. Now just give back the toy and we'll —"

"No!" The boy pulled the little ivory pig close to his coat.

"The thing is his," Okoro told her.

"To keep?"

"To keep — a gift. He is our first American."

"Say thank you to the nice man," the mother commanded.

The child reached up his arms in an innocence that, with very great luck, he would never lose. And then they were gone in a rush of glitter and fur.

"Some *people*," the guard said.

"We must find a hotel," Okoro told the others. "Tomorrow maybe we will find where Hamisi has gone. Tonight, though—" He looked at the guard. "May I use this to call about lodging?"

"Out there," the guard said, jerking his head at the door. "There's a pay phone outside."

*   *   *   *

It had come with a strange suddenness, first a horizontal blast of cold rain that rattled like pebbles against the kitchen's north window, then a curtain of snow, wind-flung and wild, making earth and sky a blind unity of white.

The barn could just be seen, its dark rectangle askew, leaning into the gale. But beyond, where the land fell off to the bottom fields and the river . . . nothing. The porch door banged and she heard him stamping to clear his boots. He came into the kitchen, his eyes watering and his face driven slack by the cold. She looked the question at him first, then, needlessly, asked it.

"None of them?" Tellie said.

He shook his head. "Not yet."

Darkness was coming quickly and, stepping to the window again, she saw that the barn had vanished altogether.

Their little herd of milk cattle had gone out in the pale sun that morning — cows with names like Star and Spot and Lame, fourteen in all — to forage for winter wildgrass in the unfenced and willow-grown roughlands southwest of the river called Bryant.

"I'm going to call Lester," he said behind her. "We can work down the back way, from his place, and maybe find them."

He was thinking that the morning's skim ice would be thickening now over the river's deep pools. Marching head down into the storm, with nothing to guide by but whiteness and wind, a cow could miss the shallows. Anything that went through ice into those still, dark holes would not come out again.

Tellie heard him in the other room — voice thin and hurried — then he came back into the kitchen and took up his coat.

"John," she said. He turned at the door. It was four miles from Lester Dekins' place down through gully-broken timber to Bryant, and another two home. Six miles on foot, on the worst day of memory. She wanted to say that there were things that mattered more; that a man, too, could step wrong in such a storm.

"We'll take care," he said, and the wind explored the room behind him.

The road to the Dekins farm wound up through oak and hickory timber to the stony upper country. Blasts of wind shook the truck and eddied inside the cab. His glove wiped a hole in the frost. He was driving, now, not by the road itself but by the memory of how it *ought* to go.

And if they're lost? he let himself think once. He could make no plan beyond that. And he could not help thinking, too: *What's the point of it? Who's a man to blame for chipping his life away, breaking it maybe, against the barren land?*

Then the gate was in front of him and he swung up near the house. Dekins was crossing to him, calling words whipped away on the gale. John got down from the truck.

"They're in," Dekins told him. "Carol's on the phone with her now."

"All of them," Tellie said, her voice distant and excited on the wire. "It lifted for a minute, and in the last light they were crossing the bottom pasture in a line. I counted." He put down the phone.

"Sit," Dekins said. "Have some coffee. Have a piece of pie. No hurry now."

"Better not," he told them. "She'll be waiting. Chores still. And they'll want feeding."

Dekins followed him to the door. "Be careful going down."

"Thanks," John told him.

"What for?"

He backed the truck and turned it. The storm gave no sign of losing force. His tire tracks were gone already and the snow had drifted level in the shallow cut between the trees. He was thinking of them pressed steaming and close at the feeding trough. Their warmth came up to him on the steep, cold road. Unreasonably, then, spring seemed near and possible, and the design of a man's life whole and clear again.

*   *   *   *

She knew, 30 miles before El Paso, that there would never be time.

"How much to go," she asked him.

"One hour," Manuel said. "Maybe less." His thin brown neck was bent forward hawklike over the gauges, urging the old Plymouth to its supreme effort. Sometimes, a long time between, the lights of an oncoming car filled their own and she could see herself, from a view of great detachment, twisted on the rear seat, her hands drawn up in fists.

The pain came again. Marea bit down hard on the folded towel to stop the shout.

"Too far," she told him.

He only leaned farther forward, rocking his shoulders as if to speed their progress. The machine rolled on at its steady 40 miles an hour.

"Faster and it will break," he said.

"Stop then," Marea told him.

"Where?"

"Here — anywhere. It's too far." The pain swept her up again.

It was then (by act of merciful Providence, he would later think) that the little cluster of lights rose up ahead and to the left, white diamond points against the emptiness of the West Texas night. A man might drive that road a year — and he had — without remembering a village there. Now he swung off the highway and along the gravel that clicked and rattled under the fenders.

"A place," he told her. But the towel was between her teeth and she made no answer.

The face of the woman looked down suspiciously at him through the glass of the closed outer door.

"My wife," Manuel said, ancient fear burning from his eyes. "Her time has come early. We cannot get to El Paso."

The glass door sprang outward.

"Arthur!" the woman shouted into the house behind her. "Go to your wife," she told Manuel. "There'll be men to help. I'll call for the women."

On the car seat, Marea saw him bending over her, felt his touch on her face. There were others then. Strong hands lifted her and carried her into light and warmth and put her on a bed.

"It's all right, honey," the woman told Marea. "I know — I know. But it's all right. We've done it before."

Now other lights, yard lights, were on between the dozen houses. Manuel stood outside with the men — out by the tired Plymouth. The others were talking, supporting him with their slow words, remembering themselves how it had been. The infinity of night pressed around them, binding all together in that little lighted place where cigar smoke curled palely and strong women hurried with bundles across the dry grass and where, in its carelessness of time and company, a child would soon be born.

Poor Folks' Ways

orning in Fouts Fork . . .

Dogs barking, men coughing, coal trucks grinding in low gear down the crooked lane off Caney Mountain. The stream ice-bearded, steep banks faced with crushed car bodies, flowing acid-gray over blown tires and eviscerated spring mattresses and refrigerators with their works gone.

Above, the mountain shading brown to blue and disappearing in a hanging cloud, untouched yet by the sun, with West Virginia on the other side. Below, the roof of Cecil Tackett's store, chimney spouting a plume of saffron smoke.

Just as the lane down Caney had been asphalt once — and still nominally was, but broken under the wheels of the coal trucks until you could drown a dog in the holes — Fouts Fork had once been a town. Up on the mountain's flank were the rotted timbers of the mine portal where, for twenty years, five hundred men a day had gone in to work the seam.

The settlement unaccountably still had a post office — a little shed affixed to the side of Tackett's store, with an American flag in a socket next to the door and a sign that told the zip code, 41542. It was hard to say exactly what Fouts Fork was now. But not a town. Surely not that.

Seeps of yellow clay from two fresh grave mounds stained the hill below the cemetery, so people still died there. And lived there — maybe sixty or seventy of them, if anyone had bothered to count.

And now came one of these, Wandie Ray, in a man's long coat and bluejeans and loafer shoes bleached pale by the acid mud, bringing her clumsy fingers and her pillowslip full of quilting pieces down the lane to the store. She kept to the road's edge, away from the puddled filth and the spray of the trucks. A girl stayed as clean as she could, even in Fouts Fork.

Wandie was 14 going on 16 — old enough, anyway, that the county had quit trying to make her stay in school. And she wasn't at all pretty, though it would be tempting to say here she was. Too skinny for that, too sallow, sharp nose running in the raw morning. Not pretty and not clever either, at least her hands weren't. They wouldn't put the needle through the cloth where she meant it to go.

That seemed like such a little thing, but it wasn't. Not according to Anna Clevenger, who had been upstate to the craft school and made quilts herself and now was teaching the rest of them how to do it.

"Coal's dead," Anna told them. "Dead as a nail. Lookit round this place. Show me a man ain't dead er sick er laid off. Women's got to carry it, cause there ain't no one else."

So they'd begun in the spring — three miners' widows and two wives of crippled ones and a girl with no gifts but a lifetime to spend, six of them besides Anna Clevenger. Three days a week they sat on the boxes and broken chairs in the cluttered back storeroom of Cecil Tackett's store. And if it hadn't been for Anna actually selling one, even if it was one of hers, the Fouts Fork Quilting Co-operative would have given up its holy mission long before the last bluebottle fly slipped into an autumn drowse on the storeroom rafter.

But the fact was she *did* sell one. The check came in the mail from a store in Cincinnati that handled country things. It was written on one of those machines that punch holes in the paper. And the numbers punched out were half a month's wages for a healthy man. They held it in turn, and then Cecil cashed it for money out of his register (knowing it would all find its way back there in any case) and Anna divided it — $28 and some change for each of them.

"Y'see!" she told them. It was August then, and the excitement made her red-faced and sweaty damp. "City folks'll pay big cash money for any kind of old common quilt so long as it's sewed by hand. Detroit City, Chicago — why they got people lined up awantin' one."

They listened to her, and they wanted to believe it. Did believe it for a little while. Then Wandie Ray would look down at the mess her wooden fingers were making with the needle and think to herself, *Lordamighty, who'd stand in line for that?*

"Keep at it, honey," Anna would tell her. "You got a real sweet pattern."

"Yessum," Wandie would say hopelessly.

"You just got to be a little carefuller cuttin' an see can you maybe stitch a little evener."

"Yessum."

"You'll get onto it," Anna would say. "It just takes a while. Us pore folks has got pore folks ways."

That was August. Now December had honed the wind to a blade and Wandie was coming runny-nosed down the lane with a bag of fresh dress scraps to make new crooked points for the same old crooked stars, most of the orignal pieces having by now been worn to fuzz from all her desperate takings-off and sewings-back.

The store wrapped her in its heat and smells. Up front Cecil's sister, Letha, was doing morning business at the wooden counter, trading food for the government stamps or writing it down in her book of accounts against some hungry family's hope of better times. The men were by the stove, and except for the storekeeper himself they were all coal miners. Or had been, or meant to be if they heard of anyone hiring.

They squatted on the empty carbide cans, coughing up little pieces of themselves from shredded lungs and shooting furious wads of spit against the glowing iron of the stove. Mostly they talked about the revolution that needed to be made — the real kind, with dynamite and guns — against the courthouse and the union and the outside money that both had bedded with to own and ruin the county. Sometimes they considered all the ways there would be to spend money when the deep mines opened again and brought prosperity back to Fouts Fork.

They had been sitting there as long as Wandie Ray could remember, their faces a permanent coal-dust gray, talking that same talk, their coughs rustling softly inside them. It was only the names that changed. They didn't even look up when she passed.

*   *   *   *

The cold draughts made a whistle coming in under the tin of the storeroom walls. The ladies of the Co-operative had their own stove and Anna Clevenger kept it banked on the days they didn't work. But on these bitterest of mornings the stove and the weather were about an even match.

Anna was wrapping brown paper around a box for shipping. It was the fifth box she'd sent — nineteen quilts in all, and that in not much more than half a year. They'd gotten paid for only four, but the stores they sent them off to wrote back nice things about the work. Wandie's starred one was folded on the chair where she'd left it. Not quite done. Never quite done. And already worn out, nearly, from all her handling of it.

"Don't give it no mind," Anna told her, double-knotting the package cord and plucking it like a banjo string to test the tightness. "The Lord'll let you finish in His own good time."

"He ain't the one keeps messin' up," the girl said.

She picked the limp thing up and shook out the folds, holding it at arm's length. She might be clumsy, but there wasn't anything wrong with her eyes.

"Do you reckon —" she began.

Anna Clevenger licked the label and smoothed it on the package. "What's that, honey?"

"Well, it seems like somebody'd almost have to have the devil in them to make an ugliness like this."

"Hush you!" Anna said. "Such a way to talk. You'll get it finished all right. An when y'do we'll send it separate, in a box of its own, so they'll be sure an notice how sweet it is."

She took the hopeless patchwork from the girl's hand and refolded it and tapped Wandie under the chin with a knobby forefinger.

"Keep yer coat on," she said, "an you'n me'll go round together an get this posted 'fore the mail truck comes."

The postmaster, Estill Ray, was Wandie's uncle. He took Anna's parcel with the hand he still had and the polished stump of the one he'd left inside the mountain when he was a boy not much more than Wandie's age.

He still liked to talk coal and missed the mines the way so many of the hurt ones did. And he was talking now with one of the Compton men from up Virgie Hollow — the middle one, Burlin Compton — who'd been off for three years to the Georgia cotton mills and saved some money and now had come back to open a little truck mine, not much more than a family hole, in a seam of coal up the side of Caney behind Fouts Fork.

"Good coal, too," Compton was saying. He was a man in his 20s whose face had not yet turned the gray color of the trade.

"More quilts?" Estill Ray asked Anna, and she nodded. "Then tell me," he said to Compton, "ef that seam's so good how come the big boys pulled out and left it?"

"Takes more to keep them happy than it does me," Compton said, and grinned at them all from under his miner's hat and lamp. "All I got to have's a livin'. There's places in there the coal isn't but thirty inches. But, hell, I'll load it alayin' on my back ef I got to."

"Insure it?" the postmaster asked Anna.

"Eight hundred dollars worth."

She said the amount slowly, proudly, and handed the money across. Estill hunted for a pencil with a point and wrote in his book.

"I always heered that was a wet hole," he said to Compton. "How's the timbers back in there?"

"Mostly gone. We're timberin' new as we go."

"You better be. How many of you's in it?"

"Not but four. My brother an me an a cousin of ours, and that Coy Slone from over by Ashcamp. There's coal enough for four." He slapped his hand on the postmaster's counter. "Well," he said, "time to go up that hill an dig me some money."

"Don't get too rich."

"Ain't had that problem yet," young Compton said. But he went out with the cocky, swinging walk of a man who had work. They heard the engine of his pickup truck growling on the steep lane.

"You sisters do an awful sight of quiltin' in that back room," the postmaster told Anna as he counted out her change.

"We keep at it."

"How 'bout yers, Wandie?" he asked innocently. "Yers agoin' out with this bunch?"

"Shame on you, Estill Ray!" Anna told him.

Word of the girl's lifetime quilting project had gotten around some, but it was no fit thing for a grown man, an officer of the U.S. government and an uncle at that, to be making a giggle about.

She hooked her arm in Wandie's. And she deliberately left the post office door open to the frigid day.

*   *   *   *

It wasn't at all like the big accidents that get written up in the news. It was one of the little ones that are forever happening somewhere up those forgotten hollows — so often that the people have come to think of them as a part of the way of life.

The Fouts Fork Quilting Co-operative had eaten lunch from its sacks or gone home to feed its men — those who had them to feed — and had pieced away the bigger part of afternoon beside the fire. And was just now, on the very day we have been speaking of, folding up its handiwork to take or leave.

The chances are that if you had been there you would not even have noticed. A low, long sound like a far-off stir of thunder, more nearly felt than heard. A trickle of fine dust sifting down from the rafters of Cecil Tackett's store. Nothing more than that. But it is the thing that the wives of mining men wait every day of their whole lives to hear or not to hear, and Delfa Justice — who was a Compton by birth — just said "Merciful heaven" very quietly and put her face in her hands. And even Wandie Ray, young as she was, knew that somewhere in its tunnelled and timbered heart a part of Caney Mountain had moved.

So they went out as they could, quick or halting, past the stove in the outer store from which the men already were gone, past the empty counter and the cash register left standing open. Up the broken lane, with others coming out of their houses too, across the timbered bridge and up a road of frozen mud past the cemetery to the driftmouth of the little Compton mine.

A man had Burlin Compton by the arm, trying to hold him from going back inside.

"How many of em?" the man was shouting.

"The whole thing come down," Compton told him, wild-eyed. His miner's hat was gone and tears ran in white streaks down the black of his face. "I was just startin' in an the wind of it blowed me clean back out."

"I know, man! But how many's still in?"

Others had him under the arms now to hold him up.

"Two," he said. "My baby brother an Coy Slone — the two of em. One stayed out sick. Aw —" His knees went and they had to catch him.

Then from down in that terrible dark hole, through smashed timbers and dust floating thick as water, the very least hint of light came probing. And behind the light there was a voice.

"Come git us, somebody," cried that voice from the dead. "I can't carry Coy no further an he's got an awful bad hurt back."

Men — young and old, crippled ones and whole — fell over each other trying to be the first ones down that hole. They brought the hurt man out and laid him on the iron-hard ground, with him begging not to be carried anymore. It hurt that much.

Under the people's feet the earth gave a final small shiver as Caney settled another fraction. An exhalation of warm inner air mixed with coal dust soughed out from the driftmouth and condensed white in the cold. The mine's last breath.

The Compton women came bouncing up the frozen road in a rusty Oldsmobile, crying and screaming for their men. On the ground, Coy Slone was passing out and coming to, shaking with shock and the cold, and the shaking would make him pass out again.

"Build a fire up close," somebody said.

The winter sun was setting, evening advancing with a rush.

"Git somethin' to cover him up with!"

What Wandie Ray could offer wasn't much at all — not enough, really, to warm a hurt man even a little bit. But it was what she had, so she spread her quilt over him, and her coat on top of it, and then the others used their coats too. At last, from the bottom of the mountain, just rounding its flank, could be heard the siren of the ambulance someone had thought to call from Clinchburg on the other side. The machine lurched up the crooked lane to the mining road, and up that. And expert hands lifted Coy Slone to carry him away to the hospital to be fixed, if that were possible.

In that coming dusk, led by a preaching man among them, the people of Fouts Fork raised a hymn of joy and amazement to the Providence that would let a mountain swallow two men and then cause it to give them back again. Then, chilled through themselves, they turned to start down.

It wasn't even Wandie Ray but Anna Clevenger who remembered the thing trampled underfoot and who snatched it up. She searched about for the postmaster.

"Where are you, Destill Ray?" she called. He stopped and turned with the others.

"Lookit it," she commanded. "An look real good. Because it's somethin' fine!"

So transfigured the quilt was, as Anna held it up to them, with the black dirt of a miner's clothes and his frozen blood, that they couldn't begin to tell the pattern had ever been stars, much less such poor imperfect ones.

Strays

I guess it hurt a lot," the waitress said.

"Some," the young man answered. "Not like you'd think."

The empty sleeve of his jacket was fastened across the front with a safety pin.

"Probably you don't like to talk about it," she said.

"No, it's all right."

It was the kind of small diner nearly everyone's been in at least once. Eight stools on chrome pedestals, Formica counter grooved with cigarette burns and ringed with spills, fry grill behind, vent fan over the grill and above that the menu — changeless as an epitaph — that said *Breakfast 24 Hours.* Half a block off the freeway and not far from the bus station, it survived by staying open when everywhere else was closed.

The two of them were the only ones in the place.

"The thing is," the young man told her, "it all goes so fast. So much noise. People running around. Then the helicopter. It doesn't exactly register, you know what I mean?"

"I guess."

"Or maybe you just block it out. Anyway, the worse comes later. When you figure how everything's changed. Crazy part is," he said, "it wasn't even a real war. Just a fight over a few miles of desert."

"At least it's your left one."

"I'm left-handed. Was."

"Wouldn't you know it. More coffee? It's about six hours old. I guess I could make some fresh."

"Don't bother. Coffee's coffee."

She filled his cup and leaned on the counter, chin in her hand, while they talked. Steam beaded and ran down the inside of the front window, and a reflection of the lights on the little tree beside the register blinked watery in the glass.

"It's a rotten night to have to work," the young man said.

"You're working?"

"No, I'm on the road. I meant you, place empty like this."

She shrugged. "Sometimes truckers stop down at the pull-off and walk up. Tonight was slow."

"Everybody else is home," he said.

Or *almost* everybody, they both were thinking.

"Where you headed for?" she asked him.

"I have a buddy in Chicago. He wrote I could stay with them."

"It's already Christmas. You're late."

"I know."

She looked past him at the window. Morning had drawn a crack of light at the very bottom of the dark sky.

"I wish it'd snow," she said. "It's cold enough."

The young man had noticed how pretty she was. There were some care lines on her forehead and around her brown eyes, but she was nice-looking just the same.

"What about you?" he asked, looking down at his coffee.

"What about me?"

"Married?"

"Twice," she said. "Not now."

"Kids?"

"Sure. A new one. You want to see it?"

"You mean you got it with you? *Here?*"

She fetched a cardboard box from the back room and opened it on the counter top. Inside the box was a gray, tiger-striped kitten. She took the little cat out and held it with both hands against the side of her face.

"Fella found it in a bunch of papers at a truck stop and dumped it here last night."

"You going to keep it?"

"Not here! They'd close the joint. I'll take it with me when I go. Kitty this small can't make it on its own."

"Something's wrong with its tail," he said.

"Yeah. Busted some way, maybe in a door. Feel it."

The tail was too short, and there were hard knots inside where it made two right-angle bends.

"Don't matter," she said, and laughed. "Cat's broke. You're broke. Everything around here's broke."

"Not you," he said, looking straight at her.

She stopped laughing and looked away.

"Me, too."

The morning had turned blue. A few flakes began to fall, and then came harder. It was going to snow, after all — a real one.

"Well," she said. "It's about time for the day girl."

He got out his wallet, opened it one-handed and got out a bill.

"You can stay if you want to. What time's your bus go?"

"Five," he said.

"That long?" She rang up his coffee, one cup. Refills didn't count. "So where you going to find a Christmas dinner?"

"Here, I guess." He grinned at the idea. "Burger, fries. All the trimmings."

She looked at him as she pushed his change across the counter. She was thinking he had a good face. You could see the hurt in it, but it was a nice face all the same. Plain and open and kind.

"Listen," she said.

It scared her, what she was about to do. She'd been wrong enough times that it scared her at the start.

"I've got this girlfriend," she said, "and we share a place. We're going to cook a real meal. She wouldn't care if you came."

"No." He shook his head.

"Why not? It's the same for three as two. You can carry my cat for me."

It scared him a little, too. But then he thought, what else was there to be afraid of that hadn't happened already?

"How far?"

"It's a walk," she said. "I've got a bunch of stuff to lug. We'll get cold, and so will the cat. Unless maybe —"

"Maybe what?"

"I mean, if you don't mind. Maybe he could ride in your sleeve."

She'd just finished pinning the kitten inside when the day girl came. They went out in the morning and the ground already was covered white.

He walked on the side the wind was coming from, so instead of hitting her straight it eddied around. It felt good to have someone do that.

They both were full, suddenly, of the amazing power that creatures and people have to make each other whole.

"Does it wiggle?" she asked him.

"Not much. But I'll tell you what's queer. Having something in there again. I don't mind that."

She felt his sleeve with the cat inside it.

"It makes me feel less broke."

"You're not broke. I just said that."

"Right," he said. "Nobody's broke. We're just nicked a little."

Side by side, breath pluming up, they left their footprints along a street he didn't yet know.

"In fact," he told her, "I feel brand new. Like everything's just beginning."

"Why not?" she said. "Isn't this the day for it?"

Waiting for the Light

The life of an itinerant journalist contains certain drawbacks, having principally to do with money. But along the road you sometimes become rich in other ways — in memories, half-memories, and a further category composed of places and events partly remembered but later enlarged by invention.

It's into that third class of artifacts that I would place my recollection of the Christmas spent with Henry Gleed, a sad and remarkable man. Pieces of the experience I am unsure of. They may be perfectly true, for even today they seem vivid as truth can ever be. I simply can't say.

But other parts I know beyond any doubt to be dependable fact, so I will begin with those.

My employer, a wire service with offices in New York, London and Johannesburg, had sent me to Nigeria to file stories on yet another in the serial coups d'etat in that broken country. In those days, heads of state quite regularly were slain and new ones installed. For a newspaper writer, reporting on the politics of Nigeria was like covering a boxing match in a ruined stadium, in which every round was required to end with a death.

As I was about to leave Lagos to make my way back through London to the States, I received a cablegram at the hotel from the chief of our foreign desk — Ferguson, I believe it was then — asking me to contact him in

New York. If for some reason a call couldn't be gotten through, I was to acknowledge by wire and wait for further instructions.

The phones *were* working that week, as it happened.

"We'd like you to stop off in Ghana on your way out," Ferguson said.

"Do you know what day it is?" I asked him. "It's the 20th. I promised I'd be home for the holiday."

"I know the time's tight. But this is something you can handle in a day, two days tops."

"And I'm getting sick," I told him.

"Malaria again?"

"I don't think so. Bad stomach. Very bad. It could be amoeba. What's the story?"

"There's been a report of a big diamond strike up around Kumasi. Their government's making quite a splash about it."

"Well, believe me, it's nonsense. Kumasi's where the gold is — or *was*. There are no diamonds in Ghana."

"Nkrumah claims there are."

"He's wrong. It's a waste of time."

"Probably so. But the South Africans are interested. The market's reacting. If there's nothing to it, they'd like the thing spiked. One day up, one back. Bring your notes with you and write after Christmas. You'll be home by the 23rd."

"That's wonderful," I said.

But I went. In this business, you go where you're told.

*   *   *   *

It's the best part of a hard day over bad roads north from Accra on the coast to the place where the diamonds were supposed to be. At least it was then. It might take longer now.

The country changes as you go. First there's the fine palm forest along that splendid bend of shore. Then scrubby brushland and little farms as you start up, Then as you gain elevation away from the sea you come finally into the true rain forest, the road a fragile track winding through cathedral stands of silk-cotton trees, the giants that rise above everything, their canopies interlaced to make an emerald twilight by middle afternoon.

The map showed an installation of some kind a dozen or so miles ahead, a one-time outpost of empire, most likely. I pointed out the place to the driver.

"Maybe," he said. "All maps old. Maybe gone."

"Let's hope not," I groaned. I was suffering greatly with my stomach.

The place was still there — two small, European-style board buildings, the boards bleached white as bone, and two huts, all huddled inside a perfectly trimmed hedge, on a rectangle of grass so smoothly mown that it might have been a putting green. The driver braked alongside a gate in the hedge and stopped the engine. The place was silent as a sepulcher. A fly buzzed inside the car.

Hello," I shouted from the window. Then again: "*Hello, anybody!*"

A slender black man stepped out of one of the huts and stood looking at the car. Then the screen door of the nearest board building clacked open and a white man in starched military shirt and shorts, with an extravagant mustache, came onto the little porch and stopped at the top of the plank steps.

He stood motionless a moment, and seemed to be composing himself — like someone trying to remember the act of speaking.

"You are?" he finally cried out across the lawn, a bit too loudly.

"A journalist," I replied. "My name is Harwell. I've come about the report of diamonds."

"Hah!" he bawled. "*What* diamonds?"

This much of it I know absolutely to be true. This much and a bit more. At any rate, the man in the khaki shirt and shorts was Henry Gleed.

*   *   *   *

Once the dam of speech was broken, he talked freely. Soon I had most of his story.

He was in his late 40s, and had come to Africa fifteen years before as a minor colonial functionary. There'd been four officers at the station then. The other three were unmarried. His wife had not taken well to Africa or to her loneliness in that place, and had gone home to Manchester. He learned of the divorce by letter.

Then Ghana's independence had come. His three colleagues had been transferred, and two of them soon left the service. He'd stayed on.

"For what?" I asked him.

"I can't quite say. To keep a presence, I suppose. They continue to pay me. So I stay."

Originally there'd been two other wooden buildings, both lost in a bush fire some years ago. There remained only what I saw — his house, on whose porch we sat; a smaller screened structure a little way across the perfect lawn, and the two huts, one for the African and the other for occasional visitors.

Once in a great while a European traveler would pass that way, usually from the World Health Organization or some other international agency, and would find the place useful as a base for a few days, sometimes as much as a week. Otherwise, he and his house man, whose name I've forgotten, were alone there.

Even as Gleed spoke of him, the African appeared with tea.

I'd spent time in that territory once before, near a village called Mampong. The people of that region are a slender folk, almost elegant, and the house man, who looked to be about Gleed's age, was exemplary of the type. As tea was being poured, my driver, who'd been waiting with the car, came to deliver a startling announcement.

"Go back now," he said.

"No, not today," I told him. "We go back tomorrow."

The car had been hired for two days, but if you know Africa, you know nothing ever is quite certain there. The driver was fixed in his position.

"Leave now," he insisted.

"Let him go," said Gleed. "He'll go anyway."

"But I have a flight tomorrow night from Accra."

"My man will drive you down. Or I'll arrange transport. We'll get you to your plane."

I'd seen no vehicle of any kind, but he said it so assuredly that I assumed there must be one somewhere. We watched as the driver backed, turned, and trailed a plume of dust back through the tunnel of the forest.

"About the report of diamonds," I said, feeling in my pocket for my notebook and pencil.

"You may as well put your book away. It's rubbish."

"That's my thought, too. But the government's making a big deal of it. My editor wants a piece."

Gleed stroked his vast drooping mustache and shook his head with a look of rueful amusement.

"It's a perennial," he said. "It surfaces every few years, always from the same area. The people there have no road. They had one once, but it's gone back to forest. They're hoping the rumor of diamonds will get them a road. Everyone in Accra knows better."

"Then why is the government playing along?"

"Money," Gleed said. "Why else? The exalted leader thinks maybe he can get the British or you Americans to give him financing for a road, which of course he'll use for something he wants more."

"So that's it?"

"That's the sum of it," said Gleed. "I'm afraid you've made a trip for nothing."

"No. It's still a story."

"Have you eaten?"

"Can't," I told him. "Bad stomach for a week now. Something I picked up in Nigeria."

"You can get worse than a stomach there."

The cramps had gotten more severe on the drive. When they came, now, I could feel the sweat pop out in beads on my face. I would go straight to a doctor when I got home. Until then, there was nothing to do but suffer it.

"So," I said, "it's just the two of you. What do you do?"

"He looks after things," said Gleed, indicating the African with a glance. "And sometimes cooks. I cut the lawn."

"It's very nice. I noticed it."

"For a time I had a power mower. It was easy and fast. But then petrol got to be a problem, so now I have the old-fashioned kind, the kind you push. It does the job nicely, but slower."

I looked across the compound, trying to imagine getting over all that with a push mower.

"Three days," Gleed said, reading my thoughts. "From here to the far end. Then I come back and start again."

"You mean it's continuous?"

"Full-time in the rainy months. This time of year I cut back to half-days. If you'd been here this morning you'd have seen the snake."

"Snake?"

"We have a cobra that lives in the hedge. He comes out to watch me mow. About a nine-footer. A civil creature — quite sociable, really. Not in the least aggressive. That's our little community here. Two men and a snake."

The variety of lives is infinite, I was thinking. There's no limit to what some people will choose, or accept.

"You're looking a bit gray around the gills," said Gleed.

"It's this rotten stomach."

"I know. I've had it often enough. Would it help to lie down?"

"I might do that."

"Yours is the near hut," said Gleed. "There's a cot, and he'll have laid out fresh linen. Have a rest, and this evening we'll go to the club for a little pre-

Christmas cheer. Gin's the best medicine I know."

It was only later, in that muddled state between agony and dreaming, that it occurred to me what he'd said. Go to what club? Where in such a place would there be a club?

*   *   *   *

"Don't bother dressing up," he called from outside the hut door.

But when I came out, Gleed himself was magnificent in a white suit and necktie, dark hair parted in the middle and slicked down, mustache waxed.

"The dress code's been relaxed since the others left," he said. "I do it just by habit."

We crossed the grass, past his house to the smaller of the wooden buildings. It was coming dusk, and through the screen I could see a gasoline lantern burning on a shelf. Inside were four rattan stools lined up at a tiny bar, behind which the African waited in a spotless barman's jacket.

"Welcome to our little place of civilized comfort," said Gleed. "It's modest, but it suffices." He turned round to the side away from the bar, screened from the eave almost to the floor.

"Rather nice, wouldn't you say?"

Twilight was giving way to night. You could see only a suggestion of the great kapok trunks, like the pillars in an immense church. There was a sense of the forest drawing close.

"So what will it be?" He waved grandly at an array of bottles behind the bar. "For a stomach, I'd recommend gin. But we can do just about anything — except ice. There's no ice. When did you last eat?"

"Two days ago, I think. Maybe three."

"So much the better! Give the gentleman a gin, neat."

We touched glasses in the lantern light.

"Cheers," said Gleed. "The best of the season to us all."

The drink slid down. The barman's face grew nearer, then receded. The room spun. And though there's no recollection of falling, it must be that I fainted on the spot. Because that ends the certain part. The rest is less dependable.

*   *   *   *

There's a memory, or what I believe to be a memory, of waking on my cot. Gleed and the African were next to me on straight wooden chairs. The snake was there too, but well to the side — the forepart of him upraised, standing against the hut wall, hood spread, but seeming entirely benign. There was no feeling at all of alarm.

The first, very dramatic sensation was the absence of any pain. You notice that immediately. Next was the hotness of the sun through the hut window. It took several moments to fix my place in the universe.

"What time is it?"

Gleed took a watch from his pocket.

"Half past six," he said.

"Morning?"

"Evening."

"Then I've missed it, haven't I? My plane."

It seemed a fact of very little importance.

"Your plane was two days ago," said Gleed. "Rest more, if you can. It's Christmas eve. People will be coming soon."

Which people? I wondered briefly. And slept again.

When I woke next the crowd was immense — village women with babies on their hips, come from somewhere out of the forest. Children of all ages. Graceful girls and boys, handsome in the way the Ashanti so often are. Old men without teeth.

All of them — practically a multitude — were crowded improbably into the hut and around my cot. One of the oldest men was burning something sweet-smelling in a clay jar beside me. I sat up and swung my feet to the dirt floor.

"Good," said Gleed. "You're awake. It's about to begin."

"What is?"

We went out then, all of us. There were a hundred people, maybe more. It was impossible to imagine how all of them had managed to press into the single hut. A fire had been lit, directly on Gleed's perfect lawn.

I wondered where the snake had gotten to.

"He's in his hedge," Gleed said, without my asking.

The noise of the crowd fell away to a hush, and the old man who'd tended the incense jar stepped alone into the light-circle of the fire. He was very tall, slender as a cane. And he now held a large bowl which he raised in both hands as he began to speak in dialect.

"I'll interpret," Gleed whispered. "That's palm wine in the bowl."

The speaker's voice was resonant and slow. Though his words were unintelligible to me, each one had richness and weight.

"He says that it is a night of great magic," Gleed whispered. "He says it is a night when men and gods are joined."

The tall man lowered the bowl, and sipped from its edge. Then bent to spill more from the vessel onto the ground at his feet.

"He's pouring a libation. A drink for the spirits."

The melifluous voice spread over the silent crowd again.

"He's saying that there are many different people, and many different gods. He's saying that, in the dark of the world, all people, whatever their gods, wait for the light of morning. And the light of tomorrow always is a child."

The tall man bent again.

"It's another libation," Gleed whispered. "A special one for your God and for the Child."

Something was being passed from hand to hand around the circle. When it came to me, and I took it in my hand, it was a doll child, cleverly made of sticks and bits of cloth.

And I felt at once strangely at peace there, and terribly misplaced.

"I should be at home," I said to Gleed.

"Yes, shouldn't we all."

The fire fell away to an ash. The people were gone. All but the two of us, Gleed and I, in the wrapping night. Then Gleed, too, disappeared, and I woke in my seat on the plane turning over the the glittering lights of the coast and tipping down in its final approach to New York.

The great mystery was how I'd gained a day. For though I remembered Gleed saying it was Christmas eve, it really was only the 23rd of December. And as my editor — Ferguson, or whoever it was — had promised, I was back in time.

I've not written about this before, or spoken about it to anyone except my wife and a couple of nearest friends. But I do think about it, especially in this season, wondering what part was real, what part less (or more) than real, an effect perhaps of the sickness, if in truth I was sick at all.

I did make inquiry, a couple of years after, with Her Majesty's foreign office, to see what more I might learn about a civil servant by the name of Henry Gleed, and about that sad little outpost on the edge of nowhere. The reply, which was several months coming, said they could find no record of an officer by that name, or of such a place.

It's possible I somehow got his name wrong. A reporter should never trust anything except what's in his notes, and I had none.

The Ambleside Continuum

In telling about Edith Ambleside I will do my best to avoid treacle — a traditional flavor of the Christmas season, but one that cloys when the carols and cash registers have fallen silent and the holiday has passed.

Edith, for her part, was a thoroughly practical woman, not given to displays of sentimentality. In her view, feelings were to be acted on, not paraded. It bothered her not at all to be thought of as eccentric, but she would have been annoyed at the obituary writer's reference to her various philanthropies. Her name appeared on the cornerstones of no public buildings. She sought no credit for what she considered to be common decencies, believing that goodness was devalued in direct proportion to the notice it received.

That, in severe shorthand, was the character of the woman whose last will and testament the attorney had gathered them all to hear. But before listening in on that, you should know something about another Ambleside, Arthur, who was widely known in scientific circles during the last quarter of the previous century, but whose scholarship, I'm afraid, has been obscured by time.

Heir to a manufacturing fortune, he had no interest in business and devoted himself instead to the lifetime study of ornithology, earning honors from several governments and the unqualified respect of his peers. The rare

Auckland grebe (Colymbus *amblesidensis*) was the making of his reputation, although his contribution went far beyond the identification of any single bird. Expeditions took him to nearly every corner of the world, many of them previously unvisited by any trained observer. In the course of a career that spanned more than 60 years, 40 of those spent largely in the field, he filled his notebooks with some 1,700 detailed sketches of birds in their native habitat, including at least three dozen species never before described.

During the intervals between the travels of his youth and middle life, he passed his time in virtual seclusion at the family estate outside Baltimore, with its extensive library and its vast surrounding lands, a rich mosaic of meadows and private woodlands. It was there, especially in his twilight years, that he penned several of his most important works.

Little was known about his personal life. And, as I've noted, his name no longer has much currency. Memory is short, and scholars of his time were less skilled at self-promotion.

*   *   *   *

Seated behind the small writing desk of the master himself, the attorney looked at the others over the top of his reading glasses.

Their eyes glittered back at him with a brightness which he knew very well had nothing to do with the season. Although a partly-ornamented tree in the entry hall and other decorations in progress told clearly the imminence of the holy day, what excited those people now were the possibilities contained in the document the lawyer held, folded and tied with a blue silk ribbon.

Refreshments had been set out: cakes and cookies, little napkins, an urn of coffee on a silver tray.

"If there's nothing else, then," said Mrs. Gray, "I'll be excusing myself." She was a small woman of much humility, with an echo of Scotland in her speech. Trained in the service of grand folk, she had been Edith Ambleside's housekeeper-cum-companion for as long as anyone remembered.

"Call if I'm needed," she said, and discreetly left them to their business. They were, after all, Amblesides. She had no place in their affairs.

In all, they were eleven — arranged on chairs, a sofa and around the library work table. And to be perfectly accurate about it, they were, every one of them, Amblesides of distant pedigree — cousins twice and three times removed, descended quite remotely from one of the two sisters of the aforementioned Arthur, dead now more than a hundred years.

To them all, Edith had been a mysterious, somewhat mythic figure, more rumor than real. Only one of the eleven had ever set foot in the house before. Only two of them even carried the Ambleside name, and that by marriage. The others, through a century's random matings, had become Smiths and Weatherspoons and Fillsons and such. But they had gone to the trouble of consulting lawyers of their own. They had done their homework. And, in such times, it's not name or blood that defines a family, but rather the law and the the hope of entitlement.

"Well, then . . ." said the attorney, adjusting his glasses on his nose.

Conversation in the room fell away to expectant silence as he untied the ribbon and spread the papers flat before him on the writing desk.

"There seems to be some preliminary comment, an introduction you might say, which I take to have been written in her own hand." The attorney cleared his throat, smoothed the first sheet, and began.

Lives are accidental affairs. As anyone

hearing or reading this will know, mine has

been a life of privilege, though not of

idleness. Wealth, earned or not, carries

with it certain obligations, which I have

done my best to discharge.

The last of those obligations, which is

the purpose of this will, is to dispose

responsibly of such assets as I have had

the undeserved good fortune to administer

and preserve.

Accordingly:

"The next two pages are typed," said the attorney. "Her wishes regarding her estate are as follows." His eyes over the glasses rims passed from one face to another, prolonging slightly the suspense.

William Filson is to receive the leather-

bound and signed edition of his great-great-

great-uncle's landmark work, Birds of the

Southern Hemisphere. *The manuscript, with the*

portfolio of the author's original drawings, is

a part of the permanent collection of the Smith-

sonian Institution. The volume passing to Mr.

Fillson is the third in a limited edition of only

15 numbered copies. The quality of the reproduc-

tions will be found to be first-rate.

The face of the great-great-great-nephew was pale as the linen napkin beside his cup. He had no interest in the quality of the reproductions.

"And?" he said, his voice unsteady. But there was no further mention of him.

"The next paragraph concerns Mrs. Lewis Erskine," the attorney continued, "and a matched set of Sterling serving pieces which evidently, on her one earlier visit here, she had much admired."

The Erskine woman pressed her lips together in a hard line, but said nothing. Uneasiness spread like a contagion among the rest.

"Trinkets!" someone muttered. "Knickknacks!"

Disappointment was giving way to anger.

"And what's that infernal racket?"

A great chittering sound had risen to fill the room. It seemed to originate from somewhere outside on the grounds behind the house. The one nearest the library window pulled aside a corner of the drape.

"It's the housekeeper," he said. "That Gray person."

"Making that awful noise?"

"Not her. It's the birds. She's feeding birds. You have to *see* it!" He opened the drape the whole way.

Earth and sky were alive with the creatures — birds of all descriptions. The dull-colored sparrows and starlings. The crimson of cardinals and sudden blue of jays. Thrashers and juncos, glossy crows, finches with the first hint of gold showing through the brown. Birds in pairs and in flocks. Birds beyond any dream of counting.

Set out in rows across the lawn were platforms like tables, but without benches. Between the rows the little housekeeper pushed a garden cart, pausing to fill her bucket and spread generous lines of grain atop each platform.

"Would you believe it?" said one of them at the window.

"Incredible!"

"*Disgusting!*"

"If you don't mind," the attorney said, "let's get on with this."

They took their places again, glumly now. And it was as before. A handsome box, carved from some rich-grained wood by people of the Amazon, for the woman who had ridden a train down from New York. An inlaid walking stick from Madagascar for the Topeka man who'd come by plane. And so forth. Lovely things, all. But not what they'd imagined.

Outside, at the far end of the long lawn, the housekeeper stood beside her empty cart. This was her favorite time, when all the tables had been filled and she was free to watch the immensity of their enjoyment.

*   *   *   *

"There is one final page," the attorney told them.

Their little flame of hope was rekindled, but only faintly.

"Again," he said, "it's hand-written."

Everything, and all of us, are

continuations of what went before. Lives

repeat. There is an entry to that effect

in the journal of Arthur Ambleside. He

also believed there is a continuity of
obligations. That is, debts must be honored
in full.
His debt was to the birds — for his
career and the great satisfaction it provided.
But how was the debt to be paid? The lives of
individual human beings are short, and he was
already near the end of his. So, being child-
less and without heirs, he provided as he
could.

The downy rustle of birds was all around the housekeeper where she stood. Overhead, newcomers turned in the sky like clouds of smoke, waiting their turn. Every day for twenty years, or half her life, she'd done this. And each time it amazed her — the luck of giving pleasure on such a scale.

The one who followed him was Dorothy
Ambleside, born Dorothy Malvern. Widow of
his gardener, she stayed on to care for him
in his later years and was found to be depend-
able in all things, including her service to
the birds. As his last wish, therefore it was
arranged — not through marriage but by a legal
instrument — that she should succeed to his
name, his house, his obligations.
After her came Nancy, who served Dorothy and
became, by the same legal device, the next in

the Ambleside line. A child of the street, raised
in the nastiest sort of poverty, it was she who
broadened the definition of the debt to include
the human sparrows of this world, desperate in
the eternal winter of their need.
I am — or was, as you read this —
the third. And as I, Edith Ambleside approach the end of this
most satisfactory adventure, I have taken care
to make provision for the future.

The attorney removed his glasses, refolded the two typed and two handwritten pages and placed them in his briefcase.

"So," he said. "It's completed."

"What is?"

"Everything," he said.

Outside, on the lawn, the housekeeper drew her coat around her, watching the birds fluff at the feeders as the snow came harder. She was thinking that when the people left she would finish decorating the tree and put the wreath on the door and the electric candles in the window, as she had always done.

Her mistress would have wanted that.

And also she must telephone the cartage company to be certain the trucks were loaded and ready to be dispatched with provisions and warm clothing to the shelters. In recent years, more and more such details had been put in her charge.

She did not know what had transpired inside. Or what it might mean for her. She only knew her duties, and that hunger was the cruelest enemy of all creatures in all places — more unjust than ever in this season.

The attorney looked at her through the window, then turned to the others in the room.

"I can assure you," he told them, "the papers are all in order."

Then he opened the door leading onto the flagstone walk.

"Mrs. Gray," he called to her through the curtain of flakes, for it was her name for a little longer.

She trembled a bit at the summons. But then she gathered herself, as she imagined her mistress would have done, and replied in a steady voice: "Coming, sir."

She shook the snow from her coat before entering the room where the fine people had been.

"There are some matters we need to discuss," the attorney said to her. "They concern your place in this house."

"My *place*?

"Exactly."

"But I know my place, sir," she told him. "I'm the one who feeds the birds."

Christmas Walkers

We found ourselves first in a
meadow — vast, gentle and unbroken.
The way was altogether new, but we
were safe for having guides ahead.
Being so short of leg we often stum-
bled and sometimes fell. And, lying
there, made angels in the snow.

I t doesn't happen anymore, and couldn't. The world has changed. But when Mitchell was a boy they blocked the public streets for sledding. The run began at the top of 50th, at the corner of Garfield beside a church, and went all the way to Woodland four blocks down — or was it five? Barricades sealed off the side street. One year the Garfield hydrant was opened to cap the snow with ice.

They thawed with cups of soup beside the registers of the coal furnaces in their houses, then went out with their Flexible Flyers to the hill again.

Night was the finest. The course took on a terrible sheen under street lamps. At midpoint the fathers kept a fire, with coffee and chocolate boiling. Sledders stopped there to warm on the long pull up. Going down they stopped for nothing. The barricades at either side went by in a blur. Sled runners made a cold whistle on the ice. They all traveled down together in a throng, their sleds motionless relative to one another, like parachutists in free fall. Four blocks in a minute, maybe less.

A boy from Highland Avenue that winter spun out from a collision and brained himself on the curb, but recovered by summer to command the neighborhood army in games of war.

Presently the open ground gave
way to thickets, and after that a
tangled and difficult wood. We might
have turned back, then — just stayed
in the meadow — but that was not
allowed. Snowsuits were impossible for
traveling in such a place, so it was
necessary to change into more practical
dress. Our toys, too, were an encum-
brance. Sadly, the ancient panda and
lead soldiers and stuffed inner-tube
squirrel had to be abandoned, left
behind in all but memory.

The Woodland druggist, author of confections, died of infantile paralysis. Which was curious, since he was of an age thought to be safe from that.

Actually, he didn't die — but was given up for dead. At best, they said, he'd be a *vegetable*. Word of a thing like that travels. Mitchell and others pictured it, each in his own way. Mitchell's preference, unaccountable even now, was of the druggist as a carrot. Some may have seen him as a beet or potato. Then, oddly, he recovered. Fully. Was back at the counter of the store.

They bought his candy and drank his cherry phosphates, but kept their emotional distance. Regarded him as a dead man among the living, a figure of mystery and faint alarm. Later, when he did die — drowned while swimming in the Gulf of Mexico — they did not entirely believe that, either.

In some houses the word *divorce* was whispered. Children vanished from class — gone off to other cities, other schools. In Mitchell's house another word was whispered, and it was *money*. He lay awake in the darkness of bed and heard them counting at the table in the other room, putting bills and coins in compartments of the brown accordion folder. Heard voices raised, and tears. And came to know in a way he never unlearned that money was a powerful and dangerous thing, always insufficient, incapable of giving joy.

That Christmas he demanded a basketball and received an apology and a promise.

And there was worse.

Traveling light, we entered on
a harder stretch where not much sense
could be made of anything, least of

*all direction. The ground was broken
now by sudden ravines, unannounced
dropoffs and dark waters running
silent under a crust of snow. From
all around, terrible as cannon fire,
came the sounds of great branches
breaking loose and crashing to the
frozen earth.*

The thing he would remember most about college — apart from some
inexpert gropings in parked cars — was the time spent writing other
people's papers. For money, of course. You could learn a lot from doing that.
It was as good as being enrolled in the course, and in some ways better.

One midterm Mitchell wrote a senior's paper on Theodore Dreiser. The
senior had means, and rented Mitchell a motel room on the edge of town in
which to spread out books and notes. He learned more in that week about
Theodore Dreiser than anyone ought humanely to be required to know.
He also learned that some people who graduate from college have almost
nothing inside their heads — which is a useful piece of information that
should be more generally advertised.

He came home then for another holiday.

There were, surely, worse infirmities than stroke, but he was
unacquainted with those. Stroke he knew about. The grandfather who
had filled and warmed his childhood now sat a prisoner in an overstuffed
chair, and his one able hand drying saliva with a linen handkerchief. When
the others all were at table, two men brought him — half carrying — and

arranged him in his chair at the head.

Speech was gone, memory impaired, legs useless, hope ended, and dignity in such circumstances impossible. Yet he was the father of them all and still, in a strange way, capable of command. For when, after eating, they tried to sing a carol of the season, the old man's shoulders began to shake and tears fell blindly from under the wire rims of his glasses. And his weeping struck them silent.

> *From time to time we risked*
> *excursions of our own — and paid*
> *for them with hurts that mostly were*
> *not large. But that was the adventure*
> *of the journey, made possible by al-*
> *ways knowing that the guides still*
> *were with us, breaking trail, near*
> *enough at hand to hear a call.*

That same night Mitchell went to a party at the house of his steady girl, and, after drinking some with her father, drove off the road coming back. It was his parents' car, an older coupe. And even while it was still upside down in the air, before it came down, his thoughts were of money being counted into the brown folder and of the likely cost of repairs.

Then he climbed out of the flattened machine, one shoulder knocked askew and hanging numb, and awakened the people in a house along that road and asked to use the telephone.

"I may have been in a wreck," he said.

He had, even then, great powers of observation.

*Coming to a place where the way
seemed most forbidding, we made a
fearful discovery. From there forward, as far as could be seen, the
snow was unbroken. Henceforth the
guides' footsteps would be their
own. That was a solemn moment, and
a lonely one.*

The first of the funerals startled and amazed him. He was unprepared
for that happening to anyone he knew.

Death came untimely and unwanted. To an uncle, and to a cousin his
own age. To former college friends in automobiles. To the parents of friends.
To people he worked with. Before very long he was going to more funerals
than picture shows. And they did not amaze him any more. They oppressed
and frightened him.

He became an expert on funerals. Baptist ones and Jewish ones and
Catholic ones; Masonic and military; fancy funerals and buryings of a plainer,
country sort. Funerals from which he went directly back to work, and
others that were followed by food and strong drink. When he was not at

the office, the chances were he had gone to a funeral. He attended them all — remembered snippets of the sermons and passages from the eulogies.

But death was unappeased by all these careful attentions. The danger grew closer. In a quick rush of years, his wife's parents were buried. And then his own.

People came to those funerals whom he had not seen in years — and some of them *ever*. Several of the men he worked for came, high officers of the company. That surprised him. It moved him. Later, he believed he understood. Like him, they were — or soon would be — the surviving generations of their families. It frightened them, as it frightened him.

But when we had progressed a
bit farther, the wood gave way
abruptly to more friendly ground.
It was a meadow again, and somehow
familiar — although unmarked, as
if no one had ever passed that way.

One either side, from the shoulders of the four-lane, snowy fields of grain stubble ran off toward farmsteads, lights in their house windows, very small in the distance, like winterbound vessels on the frozen lake of the land.

That afternoon, in another town, he had argued with a prospective client — had left his proposal shredded and wadded in a heap on the man's desk. And now the car radio spoke news that wasn't news at all.

More hostages taken. More humiliation at the hands of yet another turbaned creep. AIDS spreading. Farmers failing. More despair. All that merging fluidly into a telephone quiz game and then into the yowl of some drug-culture hymn. He switched off the radio and there was only the hum of engine, the whine of tires on the all-but-empty interstate.

Then the faint aureole of the city's light appeared low over the road ahead. Then his own street. Then his driveway, his key in the lock. And there was no more anger in him. It sometimes caused Mitchell to wonder, now, how it was that events in the world and in his own life had lost their power to lastingly torment.

> *And starting across that*
> *easy ground, we noticed behind*
> *us new walkers, wearing snowsuits,*
> *dragging ancient pandas and stuffed*
> *squirrels, stumbling sometimes,*
> *making angels in the snow.*

It had become their habit to spend Christmas Eve with friends. A curious group it was. Some of its members at midpoint of the march, some of them nearer the end. Not much alike in many ways, if observed closely. They came, all of them, with their collected sorrows and fears and regrets ticking like spring watches inside.

A tree sparkled. A fire evoked old memories. They sat at a table grown more crowded with the years. The spring of the ticking watch ran down. Christmas stories were read aloud. Songs were sung. Presently it became unnecessary even to talk.

The children slept, then. Because that place was a part of the meadow of their journey's start. And children, sleeping, make angels not just in snow but on a carpet or anywhere they lie.

In such a manner do we travel —
older walkers and newer — through
the repeating circles of our lives.
Looking always for that warm place
where we may rest, if only one night
a year, forgetting our destinations
and caring more about the company
along the way.

A Little Fiddle Music, Please

ngelo, the pawnbroker, looked at the instrument lying in its open case on the counter top.

"Where'd you get it?"

"A lady give it to me," said the boy in the torn jacket. "She had me clean out her house. It was in a box with some other stuff. She said I could have it."

The kid was lying. The pawnbroker was sure of it. But in his business you bought the stories along with the merchandise. Guns he knew. And TVs, watches, electric guitars, stereos and jewelry. About violins he knew nothing.

"Is it any good?" the boy asked.

"It's a fiddle," Angelo told him. "Not much call for fiddles. I can let you have twenty bucks on it."

"Not to hock. To sell."

"Twenty bucks. That's it."

"There's another guy I might show it to," the boy said.

"Sure, go ahead."

"You wouldn't go thirty?"

"Twenty," Angelo said.

"All right. Twenty then."

The pawnbroker took two tens out of the drawer and watched the kid go. Then he lifted the instrument out of its case. The wood was pretty. It was nice to look at. But in the fifteen years he'd had the shop nobody had ever come in asking for a fiddle.

Probably he'd been crazy to take it at all. But then again, you never knew.

*   *   *   *

"The guy's in a state," the desk sergeant told the detective.

"He get mugged or what?"

"No. He says somebody lifted his violin."

The detective leaned around the sergeant to look out through the glass of his cubicle at the man in the waiting area. The man was dressed up in a white tie and a coat with tails — walking back and forth and beating his clenched fists against the sides of his legs.

"You can see how he is."

"Have him fill out a report."

"That's what I told him, but he says it's a big deal. He wants to talk to a detective."

"Go back out and jolly him up a little."

"I tried," said the sergeant. "He won't jolly."

"OK, OK." The detective had two shootings and an armed robbery still working from the night before. "The stuff that comes through that door," he said.

He went out to where the guy in the tail-coat was wearing out the floor.

"It happened *so quickly!*" the maestro said. His lips trembled as he spoke. He looked like he might be having some kind of attack.

"Take it easy," the detective told him. "Maybe you'd like to sit down."

"Do you know who I am?"

"We'll get that when we make out the report," said the detective. "I understand you lost your fiddle."

He looked at the second man, who was dressed in regular clothes.

"Who are you?"

"A *Guarnerius!*" groaned the maestro, his voice a ruin. "You don't understand. A *Guarnerius!*"

"That's you?" the detective asked the second man. "You're Guarn— whatever?"

"No, I'm Williams. I'm just a driver."

"My *instrument* is a Guarnerius," the maestro told the detective. "You understand? A masterwork — a thing of great rarity. And in only an instant it is *gone!*"

"I went in to get a pack of gum," said the driver, Williams. "And I must of forgot to lock the car. It was a dumb thing to do."

"What kind of value do you put on it."

"Value? It is beyond price. It is my song, my life."

"Right," said the detective. "But I need to know what kind of money we're talking about. What would you have to give for one like that new?"

"*New?*" The maestro's voice cracked hysterically. "Giuseppe Guarneri del Gesu died *two hundred fifty years ago.* They don't make them new!"

"All right, then. What was it insured for?"

"Two million."

"Dollars?"

"Of course, dollars. What else?"

The detective blinked at the figure. He had paid $45,000 for his house.

"So you see, it must be found," said the maestro.

"We'll do what we can," the detective told him. "The desk sergeant will take your report."

"What good is a report," said the maestro bitterly, "when I have a concert tomorrow in Cleveland?"

*   *   *   *

Poverty is a word without precision. There can be wealth of the spirit amid even the hardest of circumstances. Behind poor doors, as in poor earth, wonders sometimes root and flower.

Maybe it is uncommon, but it happens.

"The boy has a gift," said Mr. Melendez, and Maria Cremada, the mother of Joselito, flushed with pleasure at the words.

"A true gift, I mean — not just some small facility."

It was told that in earlier years, before he was an old man, and before he was an exile, Melendez had played with the symphony in Havana. There and in Europe. It was even said that he had played before kings.

Now, in a place where all of that was unremembered, he gave lessons for three dollars the half-hour in tenement apartments, to children of families for whom three dollars was a palpable sum.

"I do not say he is a *prodigy*," the old man told Maria Cremada. "I dislike the term. But I can tell you he is gifted in a way that, for his age — which is what, exactly?"

"Nearly 10."

"In a way that, for 10, is astonishing. Believe me. I have taught many children. Some with fingers like wooden pegs. Some with dexterity, but without heart. But this boy — last week I put before him a piece of rather great difficulty, which he had not seen. 'Just try this,' I said. And I put it on the music stand before him."

The old man spread his hands, as if disbelieving.

"He looked at the music, to play it through first in his mind. He made a little smile. Then he put his bow to the strings and . . ."

"And?"

"And everything was there. Not yet of concert quality, of course. But all was in place, and more than just correct. The *feeling* was in it — as if he had been born already remembering that piece."

"So what does it mean?" asked Maria Cremada.

"Maybe nothing," the old man told her. "Or maybe more than you can imagine. Maybe everything. It depends."

"Explain to me."

"There will come a time when he must have a master who is more qualified. Not yet. He hasn't passed me, but in one or two years more. For now, what holds him back is —"

"Is what?" Maria asked.

"From where comes the instrument he plays? Rented, I suppose?"

"Yes, rented. How else?"

"For most, it would be adequate. But when the gift is real, the violin becomes the voice of the soul. He has outgrown the voice of this one."

"And for a better, how much?"

"I haven't looked. More than one thousand, I think — or about that."

"Have mercy!" Maria Cremada stared helplessly at the clutter of her cramped room. "It is like buying a car."

"Yes, it is a heavy cost."

"What about one used by someone else?"

"The stores may have one. But I would be careful."

"There is a shop on the next street," said Maria Cremada. "The man gives money for things, and afterward he sells them. Once I had to take him a pin with a stone in it, and he seemed fair."

"But be careful," said the old man, Melendez. "It isn't like buying shoes. I think you won't find a violin in such a store. Only saxophones. Where is the boy now?" he asked.

"In the street, with the others. Kicking the ball."

"Always football," the old man sighed. "He should be careful of his hands."

"He's a boy."

"Well, tell him I am waiting for him here."

"Yes," said Maria Cremada. "And then I will go speak to the man who sells used things."

*   *   *   *

The colored lights on the storefronts, and the electric candles burning in the upstairs windows, gave little cheer. In fact, they made the brokenness of the neighborhood more oppressive. It was not an area where the detective felt comfortable to go alone, with evening filling up the streets. Young men loitering in bunches on the steps of the buildings muttered and stared as he passed.

He rapped with his knuckles on the glass door of the shop, and the pawnbroker, Angelo, came around the counter. The detective showed his badge through the glass, and the man let him in.

"I was closing."

"Right, I see that. I'll just take a minute." His eyes were going over the racks of merchandise behind the counter. "You got any musical instruments?"

"Yeah. A couple of clarinets. Nice set of drums. You want to start a band?"

"Don't get smart. I'm looking for a fiddle."

"Well, I can't help you there."

"No fiddles?"

"Nope. Look around."

"You *ever* get them."

"Hey, I get a little of everything. I had one last week."

"Is that right?" said the detective. "Who brought it in?"

"Some guy."

"And that's all? Some guy?"

"That's it."

"Where is it now?"

"I don't know. It went out a couple of days later."

"You got a name or anything."

"Nope. Some woman. Cash. I never seen her before." All of it was true but the last.

"Tell me about this fiddle," said the detective.

"What's to tell? It was your basic violin. Nothing special. I was lucky to unload it."

"How much would you say it was worth?" the detective asked him.

"Who knows? It's like anything. Depends on who wants it."

"OK, then, what did you give for it?"

"Twenty."

"And what did you get?"

"Fifty."

"Truth?" said the detective.

"God's truth. I can show you the note in my book."

"Never mind," the detective told him. "That's not the fiddle I'm after."

"Let me close up, then," said Angelo. "I got a family to get home to."

"Me too," said the detective. "I guess only cops and loan sharks work late on Christmas eve."

*   *   *   *

The hall had emptied. The maestro and the conductor went out together to the limousine that would carry them to the champagne reception.

"What do you think?" the maestro asked.

"I think you were technically brilliant. But that is usual. Consistency is a great virtue, and you do not have off nights."

"About the instrument, I mean."

"Fine. I thought it was fine."

"It's not the Guarnerius, of course. But was the tone rich and full? Did I sound warm ?"

"Why yes," said the conductor. "As warm as I have ever heard you."

"Good," said the maestro. "Insurance is a wonderful thing."

*   *   *   *

Even through the closed window Mr. Melendez could hear the racket from outside. Young men were drinking on the step below. Their voices — raucous, unintelligible — came up to him like the growls of beasts.

He sat straight in his chair, the worn leather portfolio in his lap, waiting while she brought coffee.

The apartment was much like the others he knew in the district. Two rooms for sleeping, and this one for living in, with a tiny kitchen offset. It was a cramped place, but immaculately kept. Poverty might rule here, but not despair. The cracked plaster wall was nearly covered with framed prints of religious paintings and family photographs. On the table, when she brought the coffee to sit with him, was a small plastic tree ornamented with a string of miniature lights.

"You are kind to come," she said.

"It would be better to announce myself."

"*No es importante.* Someday we may have the telephone. But I am honored, and Joselito will be pleased."

"He is out?"

"Only to the store. Some last things for tomorrow."

"It is not so safe out there, I think."

He inclined his head toward the window, and listened with her to the noise coming up from the street.

"It's just the beginning," she said. "Later will be worse. Sometimes we hear the guns."

"And you worry?"

"Yes. Always. But he is clever, Joselito — clever and careful. He knows his way."

"Well, I will leave this for him," said Mr. Melendez. He put the leather portfolio on the table. "It is a small thing. Only some of my music from another time."

"No, stay! He'll be here soon. And it is perfect that you have come, because now I will also make my present to him tonight. I found one, you see."

"Found what? Not a violin?"

"Yes. From the place I told you. It seems well cared for. Better than the rented one. But you can tell us if it is good or no."

Just then they heard quick footsteps on the stairway, and the boy came in, dark hair tousled, cheeks flushed from the cold.

"Master!" he said — surprised and pleased to find the old man there. He put his sack on the counter and removed his coat. He was a slight boy, unremarkable in any way except for the curious solemnity in his manner whenever he stood before music open on the stand.

"Those ones below don't make trouble for you?" said Mr. Melendez.

"No. Why would they?" The boy laughed. "I know them all. We're all of this place."

The old man put his cup on the table and patted the leather folder with the flat of his hand.

"I leave this for you," he said. "For your pleasure."

"A gift?"

"Yes, it is the season."

The boy opened the leather binding. Inside were folios of music, worn from long use, some frayed at the folds and mended with plastic tape.

"Maybe you will try one. They are ones I have loved."

Joselito turned the antique pages with wonder and respect.

"Yes," he said. "I'll try one now. But which?"

"May I suggest?"

"Let me get my fiddle."

"I must tell you," said his mother. "It is gone."

"*Gone?*"

"Returned," she said, "to the renting place." Full of pride and mystery, she marched into her small bedroom. The boy watched her kneel by the bed, and bring from underneath it a box, which she carried out and placed beside the leather folder on the table.

"Don't stand like a goose," she said. "Look quickly."

The boy untied the box. He lifted out the case and, astonished, held it unopened in his hands.

"Not rented," she told him. "It is *owned.*"

He unsnapped the latches.

"I know nothing about such things," she said. "We must have your master's opinion."

Mr. Melendez took the violin from its case. He plucked the strings in turn. It was almost perfectly tuned. He drew the bow gently across, and his eyes widened. The old man turned the instrument in his hands.

"What do you think?" asked the boy's mother.

What *could* a man think, holding perfection for the first and only time in his life. It had no identifying mark that he could see. Therefore he could not know which hands of genius had made it, or in what workshop it had been born, or even in which century. He only knew it was extraordinary. Of that much the old man was certain. It could even be one of the very, very great ones, whose names were famous in all the world. He had read of such instruments. He had never dreamed of touching one.

The wood glowed in his hands, as if with living vitality.

"What do you think?" the boy's mother asked again. He looked at her — at her expression of hope, of utter innocence. And he said to her:

"I think it will do."

He passed the violin to the boy.

"So what shall I play?" asked Joselito.

"Perhaps this one. The *andante* only."

The boy placed the worn music on his stand, studying it a moment before lifting the instrument to his chin.

The piece was J. S. Bach's Sonata No. 2 in A Minor for unaccompanied violin, with many passages that required the playing of two strings at once.

"The double-stops you will find difficult in places," said Mr. Melendez. "There you might keep to the melodic line." He stepped around Joselito to open the window.

"We'll be cold," said the mother.

"Yes, it's a cold world," said Mr. Melendez. "But music must be heard."

The boy began to play, then. And at those first fine, sweet notes the rowdiness below fell strangely silent. Hard young faces turned up, in surprise first, then in wonder.

Walkers hurrying with coats drawn tight around them halted astonished in mid-step.

Other windows were flung open.

Fear and danger fled, and anger subsided. Sorrows momentarily lightened.

From that upper room was poured out upon the world the miracle of the violin's song — a song so measured and so pure that it resonated like the beat of an impassioned heart.

And beauty filled the whole poor street, as it would fill so many others on that night.

The Least of These

Certain details here are invented, but the essential outline of this story was told as truth. It is possible that, with due diligence, one might pursue the account to some irrefutable source — some person who was there, and who actually knew the names and perhaps shared the discovery.

But it is better, I think, simply to recount the matter as it was said to have happened, and not worry the wonder out of it. So that any child whose fate it was to be born in that sorrowing land, and then rescued from there to a different life, can imagine that the story is his or her own.

———————————————————

O vernight the weather had changed. A raw wind gusted out of the east from the direction of the sea, and Ludovic, the oldest of the three carpenters, had neglected to bring his gloves.

From time to time as he worked, he blew into his cupped hands, then rubbed them together to chase the cold.

"Winter has arrived," Eugenu said between hammer blows. He was the youngest.

"Not yet," Ludovic told him. The old man regretted the lack of gloves, but it was bearable. "You'll know winter when it's here."

"Then may we finish before then!"

"Hah!" said Pavel, the third carpenter. "We'll never finish. In a town as old as this one, the fixing never ends."

"This one building, I mean."

"Yes, but after this one there are more broken ones," said Pavel sourly. "It's without end. We live in a broken place."

Their village — a *town*, Pavel had called it, but that was too grand . . . their village was home to fewer than four hundred souls, set beside a small stream that ran down through sharply folded hills and fed after several joinings into a tributary of the Danube.

And everything about it was indeed broken. Broken by the poverty of its exhausted, steeply tilted fields. But broken above all by a half-century of dictatorship, ending finally with the lunacy of the Ceausescu era. What the communists had not stolen they had wrecked by their neglect and their stupidity.

Only now, after the madman's fall, had the mending begun.

Men of the village were cutting trees in the upper hills and bringing them to be sawed into boards at the small mill that the merchant, Emil Neagu, had established. Some buildings had fallen in upon themselves, leaving holes along the roads that were like gaps in a broken-toothed jaw. Many were past saving, but there were others that with much work could be restored to usefulness.

One of those, the one on which the three carpenters were engaged, had been the home and workshop of a tanner and harness maker. But the man had gone with his family to a place in the north, and the structure was being remade into a church — or a chapel at least — with room above for the priest.

The hope had been to finish it before the holy days, but now with the change of weather that seemed unlikely. The carpenters left their tools and their aprons where they'd been working, and climbed down with their lunch pails to sit against the stone foundation, sheltered from the wind.

The young one, Eugenu, took out his folding knife and cut a piece from his sausage and another from his bread and tossed the pieces in front of the dark crawl-hole that opened at the bottom of the foundation.

"Have you seen the she-dog?" Pavel asked him.

"Not today," said Eugenu. "But she's there."

"She's still there, all right," said the old one, Ludovic. "I could hear her under the floor. At night she hunts, and in the day comes back."

They'd seen her before as they worked. She was a dog of no identifiable sort — just woolly and nondescript as the village itself, and big-titted with milk.

"She should be having the pups," Pavel said.

"She has," Ludovic told him. "I could hear them there, too."

"We ought to name her," Eugenu said.

"I have the name," said Pavel. "We call her Lucky."

They laughed at that, as they bit off pieces of their cold lunch. It was a long time since there'd been any luck in that weary and threadbare place.

*   *   *   *

Fists hammering on the door of his shed woke the old carpenter, Ludovic, at a small hour of the night. He groaned and threw off his blankets. It was middle December now, and the room was punishingly cold.

His neighbor was at the door.

"Come see the fire!" the neighbor said, his eyes shining with excitement. "They're burning some Tigani houses!"

Gypsies spoke of themselves as Roma. But *Tigani* was the officially prescribed term for them, for it was not right — not decent, even — that a part of the country's name should be usurped by a tribe of thieves and idlers. So they were called Tigani instead.

Ludovic pulled on his trousers and boots and his heavy coat and went with the neighbor to a dirt street at the edge of the village where a crowd had gathered. Flames leapt high with a windy sound, and the brightness flung long shadows of the people against the frozen ground.

"How many houses?" Ludovic asked a man.

"Altogether three."

The old carpenter watched as the houses, which were really only shacks, began to settle with bursts of sparks.

"Who did it?" he asked.

"They came in a car from some other place. Young men who have the shaved heads. I didn't see them, but Tudor told me."

"And the Tigani?"

"Gone, all," the man said. "Some were beaten, I think. There was some talk of hanging one man."

"For what?"

"For nothing," the man said. "The usual — that they are who they are. In any case, it wasn't done. They escaped in the direction of the river."

"But escaped to *what*? Better than being killed. But to be without a roof in such weather? It's a shameful thing. A wrong thing."

"Well, I have no love for Tigani," the man told Ludovic. "But I agree that it is wrong."

"How many were there?" Ludovic asked him.

"I don't know. There was much confusion — running and screaming and falling. Maybe fifteen in the three houses. There were two old people among them. One they had to push away in a barrow."

It takes only a little time for flames to consume such frail shelters, made of found boards and tin and other gathered things. Already the fire was subsiding and the crowd of villagers had begun to drift away.

"I nearly forgot," the man told Ludovic. "There was one Tigani girl, too. Heavy with child. I saw no man beside her. If they had beaten her I think she would have had it in the street. She was that big. But they let her pass."

"Shameful," the old carpenter said again. The only consolation was that the doers of it had come from somewhere else.

Afterward, though there could be no certainty ever, he would believe that the explanation for what followed must lie in the unforgivable events of that bitter night when the Gypsy houses were burned.

* * * *

Such a morning as this one — ten degrees of frost and blowing eddies of new snow — could make even a hale man feel older than his years. And Father Iosif, who labored up the hill now, his cane scritching in the gravel of the frozen path, could feel his age in every season.

The peculiar thing to the priest was that he could remember so clearly different times, as if they were yesterday. He remembered games of soccer on the small flat field behind the cannery, and the strength of young legs that never tired. He remembered nights in the tavern. He remembered the love of girls. He remembered the village as it was.

Nearly all that he remembered had been lost.

The workmen watched as Father Iosif slowly ascended the path. Their hammer blows rang sharp as pistol shots through the frigid air. The upper floor and the roof were finished. And none too soon, either, for now real winter certainly had come. Today they were fitting windows in the lower part, the chapel part.

The three touched their caps out of respect for the old priest, who waited a moment to regain his breath.

"It progresses," he said then.

"Slowly," said Ludovic. "But, yes, it does go."

"The problem is materials," said Eugenu, the young one. "How do you work without materials?"

"We were two weeks waiting for windows," Ludovic told the priest. "They said they had no glass."

"It should be colored glass," said Father Iosif.

The old carpenter shrugged.

"We're glad to get *any* glass at all."

"Yes, but it should be colored. I once saw a little church in Galati that had lovely windows made from the bottoms of bottles — green ones and brown ones. They were very nice when the light came through."

Eugenu laughed.

"That would take a lot of bottles," he said. "I would be glad to help empty them. I could dedicate myself to that."

"When can you finish?" Father Iosif asked. "I believe the widow Popescu is tired of keeping me."

"It depends on a lot," Ludovic told him. "Materials. The weather."

"By the holy days, do you think?"

"It's possible. Not really finished," said Ludovic. "But at least in a condition to be used."

"You already have a house guest," Eugenu told the priest. "The dog under the floor."

"She's still there, is she? You see her?"

"Sometimes. She comes and goes at night. But we hear her. Her and her mess of pups."

"It's a problem," the priest said.

"I think I could get a man to poison them," said Pavel, the sour carpenter.

Father Iosif speared him with a look of reproach.

"Don't even say it. She is a creature of God, and God will provide."

"Yes," said Pavel. "In the same way He provides for this town."

The priest, ignoring him, turned to Ludovic.

"It would be a great thing to have the chapel for the holy days. What do you think?"

The old carpenter shrugged. "It is possible," he said. "We can only try."

*   *   *   *

A man hunting hares found the Gypsy girl in a piece of woodland not three kilometers north and west of the village.

She lay part way down the side of a ravine, caught in the thicket of saplings that grew on the slope. In the cold, her body — dusted over with snow — was preserved intact. Wild creatures had not molested it.

The man went for his brother and together, using a cart, they had wheeled her down to the road and then carried her in the back of the brother's truck to the office of the village constable.

"It was unlawful to move her," the constable told them.

"But worse to leave her," said the finder of the girl.

"It's done, anyway." The constable was going through the cloth bag that the men had found in the forest next to the body. It contained only some pictures and a book. In a pocket of her rough coat, knotted inside a handkerchief, was a 30,000 leu note — worth a bit more than one U.S. dollar — and some metal bani coins.

Folded with the money was an identity card.

The constable had telephoned to the nearest larger town for a doctor, but the doctor was traveling and there was no other person with any useful knowledge, medical knowledge, except the village midwife. So he had sent for her instead and the woman arrived now, bundled against the cold.

"What have you?" she asked the constable.

"I don't know yet."

"Is it a crime?" She threw her coat on his table.

"I tell you I don't know. There's been much blood."

"I see that. Leave me alone with this for some minutes and I might learn something."

The constable and the two brothers stepped outdoors and around the corner of the building, out of the wind, until the woman called for them.

"As I thought," the midwife told them. "She has only just delivered."

"She *what?*

"A birth. Followed by hemorrhage. There were no wounds — no marks anywhere on her. She had the baby, then died of the bleeding."

The men were struck dumb by the awfulness of that. They were imagining the loneliness and the fear. It would have been a terrible way to go.

"And no baby was found with her?" the midwife asked.

The constable shook his head. "These are her papers. By her name, she must be of the Tigani tribe."

"I could have seen her," one of the brothers said. "The night of the burning, there was a pregnant one with them. A young girl. I didn't see clearly — not the face. Only that she was large. It was dark, and they were running."

"Suppose she had it then, as they were trying to get away from this place," said the constable.

"And could not stop the bleeding," the midwife said. "So she weakened. The others got ahead. And she became faint — became confused. Left it, or lost it in the dark. Went on a little, then fell."

The path where the first brother had found her was narrow, uneven. It followed the stony contour of the hillside, with the ravine close on the left-hand side.

"Surely they missed her," he said, "and came back for her. But in the dark . . ."

"She went quickly, you can believe that," said the midwife. "It is like sleeping. No great pain."

The constable spread the identity paper on his desk, and read the name aloud.

"I wonder if she is the one I saw that night," the brother said.

"We can ask," the constable told him.

"Ask who? There are no more Tigani left here."

"That's true. So it's possible we can never know."

The constable picked up his telephone, then, to call for someone to do the burying. With the ground frozen, it would be much trouble to make a grave.

Afterward, the brothers went back to that upland country and searched along the path, and also in the ravine below it, until they reached the place where the woman had fallen into the trees.

More snow had fallen in the afternoon. They found nothing.

*   *   *   *

The last papers had been completed, and the American man and woman, sitting in wooden chairs at a small table in the outer room of the provincial office, clasped hands nervously as they waited. In the year past, waiting was an activity at which they had become expert.

The endless correspondence, the expense, but more than anything the hopes that more than once had flared so brightly, only to be crushed. If they had known how much would be asked of them, would they have begun this at all? They'd often wondered that.

It concluded, as such things sometimes do, in great urgency and haste.

"This came up suddenly," their lawyer in the States had told them.

"Evidently it's a bit irregular, and there's not as much information as I'd like. What we do know is that the infant is healthy."

"What else matters?" they had said.

Having been so long childless — he past 50, she only two years younger — decent health was the only thing they asked.

"I'm afraid we have to move quickly," the lawyer had told them. "There's not much time for your decision. If it's *Yes*, I can have visas and your airline tickets in my office by day after tomorrow."

"We've already decided," the woman had replied.

So now they sat in this cramped office in a town whose name they could not pronounce, in a country they never imagined they would see. Their journey was nearly at an end, and there was no more uncertainty. Only eagerness to have it finally finished.

The government woman came back into the room, carrying a large envelope.

"There are photographs in this," she said. "Also a medical certificate and some other documents."

"And something of her history?" the man asked.

"There is no history," said the government woman.

"None at all?"

"Nothing to speak of." She handed the envelope to the American woman. "A car will come for you at your hotel in the morning tomorrow. An interpreter will go with you to the village."

"What time?" the man asked.

"I think about 8 o'clock — it is still being arranged," the woman told him. "It is a trip of more than one-half day there and back."

*   *   *   *

In winter, the poverty of such a place is grinding — bearable only because the enduring of it is a habit. But then a rivulet is noticed cutting a course through the banked snow of the roadside ditch.

And, surprising as a forgotten promise kept, one day the changing season sends a wash of green up the steep flanks of the stony hills. And for a little time unreasonable expectation dulls the awareness of endless need.

It was on just such a day that the carpenter, Ludovic, coming from the mill with some fresh-cut, sweet-smelling boards slung across his shoulder, saw the blue van turn the corner, climb the narrow street and stop at the house of the widow Popescu.

He watched as the people got out — the driver and two others, a man and a woman, foreigners by their dress. He knew the purpose of their coming, though he hadn't known when it would be. The news had arrived ahead of them. In houses along the street the corners of window curtains were slyly lifted.

And in that moment the old carpenter remembered, as if it had been yesterday, the miracle of a day four months before, in the last of December . . .

This morning the three men had brought no tools. Instead of their rough clothes and carpenters' aprons, they wore shirts buttoned at the neck and mismatched suit coats over their denim trousers. They looked stiff and awkwardly ceremonial as they stood together in the room on the lower floor — the room that would be the chapel.

"To me it looks good enough," said Pavel.

Ludovic's eyes took in everything, missing no detail.

"With more time..."

"No, it's good! Only one thing more," Pavel said. "To get the dog and her brood out from under."

"Leave them. What do they hurt?"

"You hear the noise of them. Every day it's different. Louder and worse." And it was true. The pups hadn't yet been seen, but they surely were larger. At least the noise of them was larger.

"It's no good under a church."

"You get them out then," Ludovic told Pavel.

"Me?"

"Yes, you. Why not?"

"Let Eugenu crawl under. He's young and limber. Anyway, he's smaller. The hole isn't big enough for me."

"All right, I'll do it," Eugenu said.

"Then you go bring the priest," Ludovic told Pavel, who went out and along the road toward the widow's house.

The young man handed Ludovic his coat to hold. The old carpenter watched as Eugenu contorted himself to squeeze through the crawl hole.

"She's here all right," he called out from beneath. "Her and her litter."

"Can you see?"

"It's too dark. But I feel them."

"How many?"

"I don't know. Two. Three." Eugenu's words came muffled out of the hole. "I'm trying to count with my hands."

Mixed with the yipping of the pups there was another sound, a kind of soft mewing.

"There's something else here," the young man said. The shout that followed sent

Ludovic stumbling backward. "Holy Mother Mary!" *the young man cried, his voice a broken wail of amazement. And wriggling feet-first from under the building, he brought out the helpless bit of life he had found.*

The infant, naked in the frigid air, was smudged over with dirt and squinting against the sudden brilliance of daylight. They bundled it in the young carpenter's coat. Pavel returned then with Father Iosif, into whose hands Eugenu delivered the child. The old priest shook with wonder as he held it. He had served his God and his village for 50 of his 78 years. But after an eternity of evil times, only on this day — his first in the new chapel — was he privileged to witness a miracle.

They hurried inside, where the fire Ludovic had started in the heating stove chased the cold and brought out the sweet perfume of the new-sawn lumber.

"It's a girl baby," Ludovic told the priest. "She seems unharmed." A more complete examination would later confirm it.

Crowded with those other new creatures in the closeness of the hole, it had been saved by the shared warmth. The mother dog had nourished it with her own pups. The only wounds, now nearly healed, were the marks on either side of the head where, after finding it in the night, she had mouthed the infant to carry it back to her den.

"Go into the street," Father Iosif told the three carpenters. "Tell the news."

They did. And the people came — so many that the little chapel quickly filled and a crowd of villagers stood outside, some in the street, others looking in through the clear glass windows.

The old priest held the infant up for all to see, then he blessed her. There was no holy water, but a man was sent to fetch a cupful from the stream. The moment transformed it, made it holy. For that day was the beginning of the holiest time of the year.

And the child was taken then to the house of the widow Popescu — keeper of old priests and homeless travelers and other ones in need.

*   *   *   *

The people from the van were a quarter-hour, no more, in the widow's house. Then they came out together, and stood talking for several moments in the bright afternoon sun and the clean springtime air.

Ludovic, making his second trip with lumber from the mill, could hear nothing of what they said. Nor could the people in houses along the street, watching from behind their curtains.

"Tell her how grateful we are to her for everything," the man said.

The driver translated.

The widow, whose shoulders shook with her sobs, mumbled something from behind her handkerchief.

"She says it is hard."

"Tell her we know."

The foreign woman spoke then.

"We will tell her about you," she said. "We will show her the pictures we've taken of you, and you with her, and of your house. We will be sure she always knows, and never forgets."

The widow nodded, and, covering her face, she turned quickly and went back in her house, leaving the couple and their infant, the driver and the old priest standing beside the van.

Father Iosif blessed the child in parting.

"She is a very special one," he told the man and woman.

"Aren't all children?" the woman said. "Surely to us she is."

"Tell them," the priest said to the driver, "that if someday she comes back to this place there is a story she will want to know."

The van backed and turned then, and went away from there along the bending road through the high forest, leaving the people of the broken village to hope for other, if humbler, miracles.

Shadows of a Storm

(A short seasonal play in two scenes, possibly to be read aloud by members of a family or by a family and gathered friends, beginning at the holiday table and ending in the living room.)

Characters

The Father	The Mother
Older Child	Younger Child
The Priest	The Immigrant
The Beggar	Choir of Angels

(Performance requires a minimum of six readers. The Younger Child also may take the part of The Beggar. All join to form the Choir of Angels.)

Scene 1

A comfortable home on feast day. A family and its guests are seated around the table from which the wreckage of a fine meal has not yet been removed. The dining room is handsomely furnished with an antique sideboard, gilt-framed mirrors and an oil painting of a spring landscape. Candlelight sparkles on the cut-glass goblets and a silver tureen, and is reflected in the dark panes of the window behind The Father's chair. The Mother enters, carrying an elaborate dessert.

THE PRIEST*(applauding)*: Look at that, will you. It's marvelous! *(He makes a mock bow, with hand flourish, to The Mother.)* Compliments to the chef.

YOUNGER CHILD: What is it?

THE MOTHER: It's a trifle. A kind of English pudding. Well, not a pudding, really. More like a cobbler.

YOUNGER CHILD: Yuck.

THE FATHER: I thought we were having pie.

THE MOTHER: We were, but I decided at the last minute to try something new. Franklin gave me the recipe. *(To The Priest.)* Franklin's our chef at the club.

THE FATHER: It's just that we usually have pie.

THE PRIEST: Pie is traditional. *(Inclines his face upward, eyes closed.)* But let us be grateful for trifles. *(Takes up his spoon.)*

(There is silence as all try the dessert, eagerly or with suspicion — except The Immigrant, who looks at his bowl, at the laden table, at the others eating. His face is impassive, like a mask carved from polished dark wood. The trifle remains untouched before him.)

THE MOTHER*(disappointed)*: You're not eating yours.

THE IMMIGRANT: Thank you. But I cannot.

THE FATHER: It's probably strange to him. I'll bet he would have eaten pie.

THE IMMIGRANT*(laughing)*: Please, no.

THE MOTHER: I may have some Oreo sandwich cookies.

THE IMMIGRANT: I'm sorry, but —

OLDER CHILD: Can you believe this? He says he doesn't want anything else. He ought to know.

THE IMMIGRANT: The question is not of wanting, but of containing. It takes little to fill me, and if I eat more I must be sick. In the place I come from, people do not dare become accustomed to eating much.

THE FATHER *(giving a little start of alarm)*: What was that?

THE PRIEST: What was what?

THE FATHER: That noise. Did you hear it? There it is again!

THE MOTHER: That's just the window. The wind sometimes makes it rattle.

THE FATHER *(stands, moves to the window, presses his face close to the pane between cupped hands)*: Something's out there.

THE PRIEST: What can you see?

THE FATHER: Just the trees whipping.

THE MOTHER: The radio mentioned a chance of a storm. They may have said snow. A weather change of some kind, anyway. I was cooking and I didn't hear it all.

THE FATHER: I can see stars. The sky's clear.

THE PRIEST: Then it's nothing. Only a wind.

THE FATHER *(returning to his chair)*: It just spooked me is all. The radio must have been wrong.

YOUNGER CHILD *(to The Immigrant)*: Where you come from . . .

THE IMMIGRANT: Yes?

YOUNGER CHILD: What do you eat?

THE IMMIGRANT: You don't want to know.

THE MOTHER: They eat like people anywhere, naturally. Don't be rude.

THE IMMIGRANT: Please. What is rude about a question?

THE MOTHER: I just think it's impolite to ask someone about personal things.

THE IMMIGRANT *(to the Younger Child)*: In fact, it is very different where I come from. People there eat what they can find. We have a saying: Whatever does not kill you, fattens you.

THE FATHER: What he's saying is they live off the land. It's kind of like when we go camping.

YOUNGER CHILD: What kind of things do you find?

THE IMMIGRANT: At one time there were animals — big ones. But all of them were eaten. After that there were smaller ones. Monkeys and little birds. Then they, too, were gone.

YOUNGER CHILD: And after that?

THE IMMIGRANT: After that, the people ate insects.

YOUNGER CHILD: Bugs? That's sick.

THE IMMIGRANT: They are not so bad. I have eaten them myself, in the good time. Then the insects were finished, and the people ate leaves of trees and the roots of plants, until the trees and the plants all disappeared like the rest.

YOUNGER CHILD: So what do they eat now?

THE IMMIGRANT: Anything. Sometimes nothing. Sometimes clay. Sometimes they carry a stone in the mouth, which is satisfying. Often they must wait until night, when they can sleep and dream.

THE PRIEST: And pray? I hope they still remember to pray.

THE IMMIGRANT: In the past time, yes. Now, not so much. The only comfort now is to sleep and to dream.

YOUNGER CHILD: Dream of what?

THE IMMIGRANT: Different things — usually of eating. But, naturally, people are not the same. Each one has his own dream.

YOUNGER CHILD: What was yours?

THE IMMIGRANT: Not *was*. It still is. I dream that I am in the boma — it is the place where animals are kept — of a very important man.

OLDER CHILD: I thought you said the animals were all gone.

THE IMMIGRANT: Except for a few, which the rich still have. And I have gotten in among his animals, and it is night —

YOUNGER CHILD: And you eat one.

THE IMMIGRANT: No, not yet. I am not yet quite brave enough to do that, even in my dream. But the animals make droppings. And with a stick I search in the droppings for seeds and bits of grain that have passed through without being digested. Those I dare to eat. They are wonderfully sweet, and when I wake up from my dream I feel happy and very full.

(All sit for a moment, staring at The Immigrant with disgust.)

THE MOTHER *(stammering)*: Well, I just don't — who'll have — can I get anyone more coffee?

THE IMMIGRANT: Not any for me, thank you.

OLDER CHILD: I understand now why pudding's an acquired taste.

THE FATHER: That's enough. If you're going to be smart-alecky you can leave the table.

(The small argument is interrupted by the sound of the brass knocker falling with a crash against the outer door.)

THE FATHER *(bounding up)*: You see! There is someone out there. I knew there was. *(Goes to door, and opens it. The draft from the door whips the table linen and causes the candle flames to flutter wildly.)*

THE MOTHER: Who is it? *(To the others.)* We weren't expecting anyone.

(The Father can be heard speaking for a moment in an agitated voice, then he pushes the door closed against the wind and starts back to the table.)

THE FATHER: It was no one. Just some beggar. *(The bang of the door knocker stops him in mid-step.)* Oh, God!

(Returns to the door. As he opens it, The Beggar shoulders past him and enters. He is an apparition in a filthy cloth coat, a knitted cap pulled down almost to his eyes, rags bound puffily with cord about his legs and feet. A plastic trash bag is slung over his shoulder.)

THE BEGGAR: Greetings from the world.

THE FATHER: What? What?

THE MOTHER: Who is this man? He has no right —

THE BEGGAR: Which place is mine? Never mind. *(Takes a chair from against the wall and pushes it to the table, between The Priest and The Mother.)*

THE MOTHER *(shrinking away)*: This is perfectly outrageous! It's — it's totally unacceptable.

OLDER CHILD: It's totally fabulous, if you ask me.

THE BEGGAR*(to The Priest):* You're looking well. Well-fed.

THE PRIEST: Do I know you?

THE BEGGAR: I wouldn't think so. We travel in different circles.

THE FATHER: Does anyone know him?

THE IMMIGRANT: I do. I know this man.

THE PRIEST: But that's impossible. You've just arrived here.

THE IMMIGRANT: It doesn't matter. I know him very well. *(As his eyes meet The Beggar's, the latter grins with broken teeth.)* He will want something to eat.

THE MOTHER: With us? Eat with us? Oh, now this is just too much!

THE FATHER*(starts to rise):* I'll call the police is what I'll do.

THE IMMIGRANT: I would not do that. I believe I would feed him.

(The Beggar has begun rummaging in the plastic bag beside his chair, drawing out a variety of objects — a lump of moldy bread, a part of a book, bits of string, a short length of barbed fence wire. He finds what he is looking for and puts it on the table in front of him. It is a grenade.)

THE IMMIGRANT*(shaking his head firmly):* Not yet, my friend.

THE BEGGAR: Not yet?

THE IMMIGRANT: Possibly later, but not now. *(To The Mother)*: If I were you, I would feed him quickly.

THE FATHER: Put some food on a newspaper. Ill carry it outside.

THE BEGGAR: Actually, I'd a lot rather stay.

THE FATHER: Well, put it on a newspaper anyway. It doesn't matter what.

THE MOTHER*(haughtily):* I don't suppose you'd settle for a trifle?

OLDER CHILD: Fantastic!

THE BEGGAR: Why not? When you're hungry, even the smallest charity is welcome. (*In a sing-song voice*): Give the beast his trifle . . . Calm him with a trifle.

THE IMMIGRANT: Save some, because there could be others.

THE FATHER: Surely you can't mean it.

THE IMMIGRANT: Oh, yes. We're just the first.

THE MOTHER: Why don't we take our coffee in the living room by the fire.

THE FATHER: There's brandy if anyone wants it.

(*All rise from the table, The Beggar with his trifle on a newspaper, pulling his plastic bag behind him on the floor, the others carrying their saucers and cups. Passing slowly together toward the next room, they become a Choir of Angels, singing to the melody of "We Three Kings," but at the tempo of a dirge.*)

"*Sad the mother, hungry the child.*
Sweet the gifts of mercy mild,
A trifle's fine, so wait in line
While keeping your knife blades filed.
Oh-oh...
Days of anger, nights of fear,
Something dark is drawing near.
Bolt the door and hide the silver..."

(*Voices fade.*)

Scene 2

*A cheerful fire sends out light and warmth from the hearth. The room is high-ceilinged
and airy, with art on the walls and many large windows. French doors lead to an outer
porch. In one corner of the room is an exquisitely decorated evergreen tree. Under the
tree are expensive presents — a new television, a computer, various toys and appliances
— and the torn remains of colorful wrappings. The family and guests are seated in chairs
and couches, except for The Beggar, who squats on his haunches in the center of the room,
attempting to eat his trifle with his fingers from the newspaper spread on the carpet.*

THE PRIEST: I hope you know how pleased I am to be here. Pleased
and grateful.

THE MOTHER: No, the luck's ours. You must get lots of invitations.

THE PRIEST: Well, as you can see — *(patting his stomach)* — I don't miss
many meals. But it's not just that. The joy is sharing this season in a happy
house.

THE MOTHER: It's true. We are happy. Life has its moments, of course.
(She looks with distaste at The Beggar, squatting in their midst.) But, all in all, yes, we
can't complain. We have our health. We have our children.

THE FATHER: And the market came back 100 points last week.

THE IMMIGRANT: Excuse me. The market in what?

THE FATHER: The market in — *(The question confounds him.)* Why, the
market in everything.

THE BEGGAR *(raising a moist pinch of trifle, as if in a toast)*: To the market!

THE FATHER *(joined by the others):* To the market.

THE IMMIGRANT: In my country, too, we once had a market.

THE MOTHER: If he says anything ugly, I won't listen.

THE IMMIGRANT: That was in the good time. Before the rains ended. And before we became so many.

THE PRIEST*(irritably)*: Population has nothing to do with it.

THE IMMIGRANT: As you like. But in those times the market was very wonderful. You could find everything there. Herbs, fruits, even fish and chickens. But what I remember most — from when I was a child — is the monkeys. The hunters would catch them in the forest and bring them on market day. They were like little men, with their skins off and a surprised look on their faces, hanging by their hands tied to a wire.

OLDER CHILD: Gag me with a spoon!

THE IMMIGRANT: Beg pardon?

THE MOTHER: I knew it was going to be awful.

THE FATHER: Let me freshen that. *(Pours from a carafe into The Priest's glass.)*

THE MOTHER: Now! Could we talk about something pleasant?

THE FATHER: I'm interested in what you said about it not raining.

THE IMMIGRANT: Never, any more. Not in 15 years.

THE FATHER: Lord what a resource! No winter, and no rain. You could build golf courses, and if there was underground water for the sprinklers you could play 365 days a year. It could be another Hawaii — better, because Hawaii gets a lot of rain.

THE IMMIGRANT: It's a novel view.

THE FATHER: Well, why not? If you people had any gumption — *(He stops abruptly, and inclines his head, listening.)* There it goes again. Do you hear it? *(The rattle of the many window panes makes a faint, unsettling tintinnabulation in the* room.)

THE PRIEST: The wind again.

THE FATHER: Maybe. But it sounds different, somehow.

THE BEGGAR (*noisily wadding up his newspaper, wiping his mouth on his sleeve*): I'm finished. What else is there?

THE MOTHER. That's all, I'm afraid. I plan to freeze the rest.

THE BEGGAR(*under his breath*): Harpy.

THE PRIEST: If your people don't keep animals and don't farm, what do they do?

THE IMMIGRANT: They build the boats. They gather stones for throwing. They prepare for the time.

THE PRIEST What time?

THE BEGGAR: The ignorance in this room is absolutely stunning. Tell them.

THE IMMIGRANT: The time when everything changes.

THE PRIEST: The Millennium, you mean.

THE IMMIGRANT: In a manner of speaking, yes.

THE FATHER(*leaping from his chair*): Now don't tell me that was the wind!

(*The beggar has begun to search again through his plastic bag, which he brought with him into the room, flinging out collected trash and filth onto the carpet. He finds more grenades, and a machete. And parts of an automatic rifle, which he begins to assemble.*)

THE FATHER (*continuing, greatly agitated*): I saw it! (*Points at a window, and at the French doors.*)

THE PRIEST: Saw what?

THE FATHER: Shadows.

THE MOTHER: Of the trees moving. Don't you just hate soft maples? Tomorrow there'll be branches all over the yard.

THE FATHER: Not trees, damn it. Shadows of things moving — people moving.

THE BEGGAR *(to The Immigrant)*: Now?

THE IMMIGRANT: Not quite yet. But soon.

THE FATHER: See for yourself. *(His face against the pane.)* So many of them.

(The others join him, peering through the dark glass of the French doors.)

THE FATHER: Where did they all come from? What do they want?

THE PRIEST: I don't see anything.

THE MOTHER: Maybe the radio said wind. I should have listened closer.

THE PRIEST: Anyway, there still are stars. It may blow a little, but there won't be a storm.

(The sound of rattling at the windows and doors has increased in ferocity until the house itself seems almost to be shaken. The presents under the tree come noisily to life: The television playing a strident game show, the computer beeping and buzzing, flashing the targets of a war game; a portable stereo booming rock music; a mechanical dog barking; a new toaster popping up toast. All turn from the glass and, joined by The Immigrant and The Beggar, become again a Choir of Angels. Above the din, the choir can be heard singing

merrily, and to the tune of "God Rest Ye, Merry Gentlemen"):

"Keep safe this happy family,

Let trouble stay away.

Preserve our goods and property

From those who cannot pay.

Build high the wall. Make strong the gate

So we need never say:

What's become of our comfort and joy,

Comfort and joy,

What's become of our... ""

(The voices of the Choir of Angels are drowned by the rising clamor from without.)

Gifts

rom far down the gravel road, from out of autumn's silence, an ancient car appeared with a small, homemade camper trailer in tow, raising a rooster tail of dust behind.

Car and trailer descended the hill west of the creek, rattled across the iron bridge then slowed and stopped on a level place of sand and shale beside the road, on whose far side a young man had just stepped from the edge of the woods.

In one hand he carried a .22 rifle, and in the other a pair of rabbits for the pot. He could see there were two people in the car — an old man and a white-haired woman, her hair pulled up in a knot behind.

The two sat talking for several minutes. Then the old man got out and unfolded a large paper, which may have been a map, on the car's fender. He looked at the paper, and then back along the road in the direction from which they had come, then back again at the paper.

The hunter, whose name was Ken, wondered what reason they had for stopping there, for it was a narrow, little-used road. Traffic seldom passed that way.

Well, it was none of his business anyway, he decided. He turned with his rifle and rabbits back through the woods toward his own cabin. Oak leaves rained down through the golden light of the October late afternoon, and as he walked he was thinking of the supper he would make.

The next morning he saw that the trailer had been unhitched from the car and the people still were there. But the mystery remained. What had brought them? He didn't have to ask. The information was delivered with a knock on his cabin door.

"We got no water," the little man said. "The agent told there was a well, but if there is I can't find it. So we got no water except what we carried with us, and that's gone."

He was past 70, a knobby, wizened fice of a man, drawn fine by hard luck. Those were the first words out of his mouth, and Ken looked back at him, astonished.

"Just so you'll know," the little man said, "we're the Monsons — Everett and Della. New neighbors, I guess you'd say. We've come from Oklahoma, and *we mean to stay*." This last as if expecting argument.

It turned out they'd bought the forty acres across the road. Contracted for it by mail, sight-unseen. At ten dollars an acre, anyone could buy the land then. That's what useless country ground was selling for. And *useless* that piece truly was. Out by the lane, where they'd pulled the trailer in, there were some openings among the trees. But the interior was such an impossible wilderness of vines and saplings and fallen limbs, so dense and tangled, that Ken had given up even trying to make his way through there to hunt for table meat.

The little man was a talker. His wife was ten years older, he said, and had worn out three husbands before him — a fact he mentioned with wonder and respect.

"I haven't seen no stock grazing anywheres close, so I guess I could dip outa the crick," Monson told Ken. "But Della's stomach's been kinda bad, and I'd rather she got good water to drink."

Ken had a well out back of the cabin.

"You're welcome to use that while you're getting set up," he said.

So the little man crossed the lane to Ken's place every second day, and filled two five-gallon plastic jugs at the hand pump. And while he was there, he never failed to come in and sit for a while, sometimes a considerable while, telling stories and rolling smokes from a pouch of Bull Durham.

"I been exploring around the place," he told Ken. "If you get a chance, walk over and have a look at what I've found."

"Thanks. I'll do that."

Monson hesitated in the doorway, then turned.

"Couldn't help but notice your machine there," he said, indicating the typewriter on the plank table next to the wood stove. "You any good with it?"

Ken laughed at that.

"Well, some days worse than others."

"You must write a lotta letters."

"Now and then. Mostly other stuff."

"One of these days, if you don't mind, I'll maybe ask you to write out a couple for me, to let some people back home know how it's worked out for us."

"Okay," Ken said. First he was the supplier of drinking water, and now a personal secretary.

"Good. So come on across an' see what I found."

*   *   *   *

From the look of him, you wouldn't have guessed him capable of a real day's work. But with only a machete and a hand ax the little man had managed to hack a network of trails through his wilderness. And in doing that, what he had discovered was a settler hut, or the ruin of one.

How old it was could only be guessed. Certainly most of a hundred years. For it was built of rough-sawn native oak boards, turned silver now with great age and weather. The nails that held it more or less together were of the square hand-forged kind.

Wild grape vines had found purchase in cracks between planks and in the empty eye-sockets of the windows, and over time had grown from delicate tendrils into wrist-thick cables. By their sheer weight, and with the irresistible patience of all wild places, they had nearly dragged the humble edifice to earth.

Everett had cut away the greater part of the foliage and made a clearing around the wrecked shack.

He led Ken inside. "Lookit it," he said. "What d'ya think?"

A single room it was, perhaps 12 feet by 16. Not much bigger than the trailer out by the road. The floor was bare earth, with no sign it had ever been planked. What remained were only a few artifacts of a spare life — shards of broken Mason jars, a blue-enameled metal coffee pot rusted through its bottom, a broken washboard.

"It's an old-timer," Ken said.

"I know that. But I can fix it up."

"For what?"

"To live in," Everett told him. "Trailer's too small. We need more room bad."

"It's pretty far gone."

"I've knowed folks that's lived in worse. And you know what else I've found?"

"What's that?"

"The well," the little man said.

"So there is one after all."

"Yep," said Everett. "Might be you'd help me clean it out. Top's all rotted an' fell in. Got all kinda c'ruption down it. Boards and snakes and bones. Maybe worse."

Ken guessed he might be game enough for snakes and bones. It was the *worse* he was leery of.

It was November now, and the wind made a sound like walking in the trees.

*   *   *   *

The little man was able, unaided, to raise one partly fallen side of the hut. And then, by levering with poles and by the use of ropes drawn through pulleys attached to trees, he managed somehow to winch the whole structure, shrieking, into square. A building again. He found cast-off sheets of tin for patching the roof, and windows from other fallen houses elsewhere in the neighborhood.

From the porch of his cabin across the road, Ken could hear the patient rapping of the hammer. Deep into autumn, now, Everett was racing the season. His hope was that they could move from trailer to the house he'd made, however cramped and cobbled, before the hard weather. And, by luck, the weather held fine.

But then his wife took an illness. Some days she would walk bent sideways with pain. Other days she would not leave her bed.

"*Colic,*" Everett would say. And later, "*An ulcer for sure.*"

His work restoring the shack consumed him, and much of the time she was alone. She could use some company, Everett told Ken. So there were afternoons, when his writing for the day was finished, when he crossed the road to sit in the trailer and hear a story she might tell.

She had lived a long time and seen amazing things. "*Oh, it's there to talk about,*" she would say. "*So much — no place to start.*" In the slitted light from the ventilator beside the trailer bunk, she was just a narrow silver tracing of forehead and nose and chin and folded hands and bent knees to the end of the mattress.

On a shelf nearby, her wind-up clock could be heard ticking, loud and quick.

"Please, I'd like to hear."

"*So much,*" she would say again. "*No beginnin' — no endin'.*" Then her face would turn in the light and her hands would begin to move, touching and going away and coming back to touch at the fingers, and into the distant, dry tiredness of her voice he would hear music coming.

"*Well, there's a sod house. You know Oklahoma, boy? A sod house to begin. And I remember an Indian boy — pretty, long face. And wagons a-goin' and the stream of ferns and the everlastin' spring comin' out from under the big rock. There's a dress and there's child pain and there's a sickness and a fire and there's a wagon to Kansas. Oh, there's a red afternoon, burnin' in the flat places, and the bluestem over the wagon wheels and — oh, Lord!*" Her voice bursting strong. "*So much!*"

In the stillness, then, the clock would tick, all her music spent or sadly changed.

"She's buried three before me," her Everett would repeat, convinced of her durability. For her pain he would bring her bottles of patent antacids, but when the sickness is cancer of the stomach those do not provide relief.

By May she would be gone. Soon after that he would reattach the trailer to the car and drive away to somewhere. Someone else would buy the land and quickly burn the hut and raise a new house in its place. Those people's brief stopping here would be as something imagined.

But that would be the ending. Now they were only beginning. "*You'll hep me clean the well,*" Everett told Ken — a statement, not a question.

*　　*　　*　　*

Eighteen feet straight down, Ken went. Down the hand-dug hole, laid up with rocks around, and the opening at the top appeared to him no larger than a bright quarter — no, smaller than that. A dime.

Eighteen feet on a knotted rope, the walls slippery with seeping water, bits of crumbled earth and pebbles raining off the edge, until finally he was waist-deep in what they hadn't managed to draw out by bucket from above: the dead snakes, the bones, the *worse.*

"*How is it?*" the question echoed down.

"Pretty awful."

"*Well, be keerful of the damps.*"

"What are the damps?"

"*A kinda gas. Can't see 'em, but they kin kill you 'fore you know it.*"

"Great!" Suddenly working faster with the bucket. "How can you know if they're here?"

"When you quit answerin' back."

*   *   *   *

The neighboring was not all one-sided.

"How's your woodpile," Everett asked.

"Getting low," Ken told him. "I haven't been keeping at it like I should."

All he had in the way of tools were a single-bladed ax and a Swedish bow saw. And his stove, an old, drafty one made for burning coal, not wood, had a ferocious appetite.

"Well, hard weather's a-comin'," the little man said. "But I cobbled t'gether somethin' we can work with."

It was a fabulous apparatus — a kind of primitive cartoon of the expensive machines you sometimes saw in the big hardware stores and farm catalogs.

A circular saw blade most of two feet across was linked by a pulley and belt to a lawnmower engine, all mounted on the front end of what looked to be the frame of a garden hand-plow. A metal bar welded to the underside served as an axle for two rubber-tired wheels on which the contraption could be propelled.

The thing looked both wonderfully ingenious and terrifically dangerous. Ken wondered where Everett had managed to scavenge the parts for his outlandish creation.

"I just poke around," he said. "Dumps an' whatnot. People throws stuff away — good stuff."

The nights were still and frosty. More than once Ken heard the mingled voices of passing geese. Stepping outside his cabin into the dark and cupping his hand to his ear, he followed the cry of them receding to the south. If the sky was clear, sometimes he could see their formation silhouetted against the silver disk of the full moon.

Morning sun melted the rime from the forest's oak leaf floor. And the days were good for working outdoors. Until mid-day, Everett hammered and sawed. And Ken sat at his typewriter, putting words on paper. In the afternoon the two of them joined forces to make stove wood.

Harnessed like mules, they would wheel Everett's monstrous engine into the woods, manhandling it across washes and around fallen branches. Always the engine was hard to start, and they took turns yanking the pull rope and cursing.

Once the great toothed disk of the blade came loose from its moorings and spun away with a *whoo-opping* noise to lodge in a standing tree. Sometimes the drive belt broke, and they would ride in the old man's car — Ken had only his feet for transport — to a salvage yard out by the highway for a replacement.

"It ain't perfect," Everett said.

"No. But what is?"

And, in spite of these difficulties, they were building two great stacks of firewood — one outside Ken's cabin, the other across the road next to the little structure that seemed now less a shanty than a living place reborn.

The old man pronounced his project nearly finished. What he had accomplished was not fine craftsmanship by any means — not cabinetry. But

Ken thought he had never seen any work more brave. That's how the days went, far along into December, with no sign yet of the bitter winter they knew must come.

"We caught us some luck," Everett said, as they came in from the woods at evening carrying empty gas cans.

And they *were* lucky, if only with the weather.

*   *   *   *

Their plan was to be moved from the trailer into the little house before the worst of it overtook them — by Christmas if possible. And with Ken's help they made it, but only barely.

Then a storm front rolled down from the north and west — a towering bank of cloud so dark it turned middle afternoon almost to night. First it spilled a spit of rain. Then the temperature plunged, and the rain changed to a snow like none in memory.

By morning the world was unbroken white, the depth of it to a tall man's knees. Cedar branches bent to earth under the weight. Where the road had been was just an unmarked levelness, with no demarkation between the lane and the ditches.

Ken heard Everett stomping snow from his boots on the cabin porch. The little man had broken trail through it, and his coveralls were white almost to his waist.

"Come sit," Ken said. "Get warm. The coffee's hot."

"I will. It's a sight out there." He wrapped his bare hands around the hot cup.

"How's Della doing?" Ken asked him.

"Better. A whole lot better."

It happens, sometimes, even with a terrible sickness, that there are such unexplained reprieves.

"I guess you know what tomorrow is," Everett said.

"Yes, I do."

"Well, she told me to ask if you'd want to come across and take Christmas dinner with us."

"It'd be too much," Ken said.

"No, I'm tellin' you. She's doin' real good. I knew she would. The only trick, snowed in like we are, is going to be findin' a bird. I heard on the radio the county had the plows out, but they aren't here yet," Everett said. "An' it won't help me none anyhow. Car's buried to the fenders where it sits."

"It's apt to be there a while," Ken told him. "Let me think on the bird problem."

It was past midday when the plow went by. Walking was easy on the packed lane after that. Ken hiked the two miles to the farmhouse of a woman he knew kept chickens, and came back with a fat hen that he delivered across the way.

Della met him at the door, standing straighter than he had seen in weeks — an angular woman a full head taller than her man, high sharp cheek bones and forehead creased by remembered pain, or maybe not only remembered.

They sat together in the one room of the house the little man had remade by force of will, at a table he'd pieced together from scrap boards, in chairs other people had discarded because of broken legs that now were replaced.

The hen was baked to a golden crust, the cornbread stuffing spiced with berries and pieces of dried fruit gathered from the forest.

And as is everywhere customary, there were gifts.

The gift Everett had given Della was this place where they would spend what remained of their days together.

The gift she gave to Ken was two pint jars of jelly made from the wild grapes that had ripened in that wilderness only weeks after the car and the little trailer had topped the hill, crossed the iron bridge and come to rest in that place.

The gift Ken gave to them was the story he had written the night before — this story you have just been reading, lacking only the end of it, which he did not yet know.

"We've got everything," the wizened little man declared.

And it was true. They *were* together still. They had a warm home. They had wood enough to see them through the winter. The water from the well was clean and sweet.

"Lookit us. We're sure the lucky ones!" Everett said, spreading his arms wide, as if he held the world.

And true or not, on that day shouldn't everyone be allowed to believe it's so?

Reunion

D on't discount, ever, the power of memories saved.

The old house leaned against the sky, atop its hill in a reach of country that progress had nearly emptied of living souls. Its boards were weathered silver; its windows glassless; its porch roof fallen on a slant. Thickets pressed around it, and parts of antique machines lay rusting in the weeds. In the gullied pasture that used to be a field, foxes made a den and hunted mice.

Sometimes a young man came on foot across the broken fences and tumbled stone walls to run his trap line along the creek below, as he was doing now. Muskrats were what mostly he caught, more rarely a mink. This day his sets all were undisturbed. He took off one mitten and got a knobby winter apple from his pocket. Then he brushed the snow away and sat a while on a stone ledge beside the stream, eating the apple, watching the twilight turn lemon-colored behind the trees, before the mile walk to where he'd left the car at the road.

The young man was only a little past being a boy, and knew almost nothing yet about losses. So he still could take a dead creature from the trap without reflection or regret. His thoughts only ran ahead, never back. He was thinking of tomorrow — the food, the presents to be given and gotten, the endless, tiresome talk of all the family gathered, brothers and sisters home from other places, the game on television.

It occurred to him he might not be able to run his line again tomorrow, and maybe he should trip all the traps with a stick. But be decided to leave them set. A walk would be welcome at the end of the long day. He stood up in the last of sunset and started back, and that was when he thought he saw a light in a window of the house on the hill.

Coming up out of the stream bottom and across the lower end of the field, he looked back again before he crossed the ruined stone wall. It was a light for sure, he could tell now in the almost-dark. And the sharp smell of wood smoke came clearly to him, carried down on the evening wind.

"The Pryor place," his father said when he told about it later — still called, as abandoned country houses often are, by the name of the first people who lived there and owned the land. "Probably hunters camping."

"On Christmas eve?"

"Hunters, or more likely tramps — drifters. You can't keep them out of those old places. That one's been empty since before we moved to town. They've ripped up boards and built fires right on the floor. It's a wonder they haven't burned it before now."

*   *   *   *

Walls and floors and the spaces they enclose also must remember. At least there's a fair body of evidence to that effect. And in certain times the force of those memories can be as strong as life itself.

Now the big iron kettle on the stove top began to steam. She opened the fire box and put in more wood.

"Do you suppose two big hens will be enough?" she wondered aloud.

"Or might we need three?"

"Two's a-plenty, if you ask me."

Startled at the voice, because she'd thought she was alone, she turned and saw her mother in a chair beside the cold-room door, a sweater pulled close around her shoulders.

"I didn't know you were here," she said.

"Tonight? Where else would I be, I'd like to know?"

"Well," she said, "I'm arguing with myself between two or three. For eight of us tomorrow — nine I mean."

"How do you make *nine?*"

"All right, there's the kids and us. Five, with you. And then there's —"

"The others can't all be here," her mother said. "You know they can't."

"They *will too*," she insisted.

"But there was a war. There was sickness, and accidents."

"Doesn't matter. *We're* back, aren't we? Why wouldn't they be? And just to be safe, I think we'll need three hens." Her voice was firm. "Ernest," she called upstairs. "Take the lantern, will you, and go out to the coop. The water for scalding's about ready. Get the two gray-speckles and the brown one. They're the fattest."

"Alice, honey. He can't do it. You don't have a man no more," her mother said. "He's gone — fell down a well."

"*Not yet!*" she replied sharply. "That hasn't happened yet. You, of anyone, ought to know. Ernest Pryor!" she called again. "Get yourself down here. I need you."

And they heard the creak of the chair as he got up. Heard his deliberate footfalls alive as anything on the stair.

*   *   *   *

"To tell the truth," said the one called Mister Aylward, "I never felt quite right about it."

"Well, you shouldn't have either?' Alice told him. She spoke her mind straight out.

"Now that's not altogether fair," her husband said. He always was the peace-maker. "It wasn't Mister Aylward's fault. It was my carelessness. I didn't know the well-top boards were rotten. I just stepped wrong."

George Aylward had been the banker. He wore his collar buttoned high around his neck, and little wire glasses that made his squinty eyes seem bigger.

"You know," he said, "I don't think I ever felt so bad about calling a note."

"You had to," Ernest told him. "I understand that. You were just doin' business."

"Yes, but I hated it all the same. With your two little kids and all. It was hard to do. And you know," he said, "I think the worst mistake I ever made was not selling the place right then."

"I thought you'd have liked it when you moved out here."

"*Liked?* I loved this place. You built it good. I saw how the boards were joined, with all the corners square. And how you'd cleared the field of stones and laid them up in that pretty wall — a wall as neat and regular as the ledgers we bankers keep. I thought of all the work that must have been, and I felt almost like I knew you. Anyway, it seemed to me you'd have been someone I'd have liked to know."

"And yet you say you wish you'd sold it."

"Yes, because people still had money then, you see. There were chances. And if I'd sold it, I might have laid a little something by. But I didn't look ahead — didn't see what was coming."

"Who does, ever?"

"Then we had the Big Crash. And everything went. The stocks I had, this place, the bank itself — everything. Just gone like smoke. I guess I must have been the most hated man in town. I heard the things folks said. It got to where, when I walked down the street, I was afraid to look at people I'd known all my life. I could see what was in their eyes. It just got to be too much, finally — more than I could take. And I did what I had to do."

"Well, you're here now," Alice said. "And it's all right. It's your place, too."

"Harriet's out in the buggy," George Aylward said. "I wasn't sure how welcome we'd be."

"Bring her in, then, for heaven's sake. You might as well stay for tomorrow. But you can't act the big-shot banker here. Take off your tie and collar and be at home."

"If it's all the same," he said, "I'll keep the collar on. It makes people embarrassed, sometimes, to see the marks."

"Ernest," Alice called from the porch door. "Can you hear me? We'll need a fourth hen sure."

*   *   *   *

It stormed in the night, and in the morning the world was white. Drew came up from the cedar grove behind the barn, pulling the fresh cut tree in the snow behind him. Then he stood in the kitchen, huffing from the cold, slapping his gloved hands together.

"It's a wonder!" he said.

"Did you find a nice one?" Harriet Aylward asked.

"I mean it's a wonder just to do that again. It seems so long."

"Not just seems," said the banker's wife. "It's been, what? Almost twenty years for you."

"Go back out and stomp your boots," Alice Pryor ordered him. "Or it'll be another lifetime before you come tracking into my kitchen." Then, to no one in particular, she said: "This is getting out of hand."

But Drew wasn't listening.

"I mean, it's like an unbelievable feeling to wake up in the room where you were born, and find nothing has changed. Nothing!"

"I remember now," said the banker's wife. "Your mother was expecting you when they took over the place from us. They came out in the car, and I showed them around. I cried the whole time. I remember her saying, `And here's the baby's room' — as if she already could see it in her mind. Though it was just my old sewing room then. They were such a nice young couple."

"I guess they were young," Drew said. "It all went by so fast."

"What ever became of you and the Miller girl?" asked Mrs. Aylward.

"Became of us? Why, nothing did. We just grew up."

"And you went to college, if I remember right."

"Colorado," he said. "I was going to be an architect. And after college to Vietnam."

"I don't know what that is."

"Just a place," he said. "A lot of us went there."

"It's certainly been a long time," Harriet Aylward said, looking at how tall he'd grown. "I guess your folks won't be here. They're still in the world, aren't they?"

"Yes, they're in Omaha."

"It would have been nice to see them."

Alice Pryor was banging oven doors in an alarming way.

"All this gabbing gets me nervous," she told them. "Drew, you get that tree shaken off and inside. The girls have the popcorn strung for it. And Harriet, I know you're a grand lady, but maybe you could find some way to make yourself useful in this kitchen."

The house was filling up with splendid smells.

$$* \qquad * \qquad * \qquad *$$

"I guess the one thing I don't understand," Ernest Pryor said, "is how you could just let a good house go."

"Now don't start something," Alice warned him.

"I'm not. I'm just curious is all."

The wreckage of the meal still was on the table before them: the carcasses of the birds, mashed potatoes congealed like putty in the bowl, the remains of three kinds of pie. And the talk had the lazy, contented rhythm of summer talk, or talk you hear in dreams.

"It was economics," Karl Kircher told him. "Economics, pure and simple." Kircher had been the man who lived there last.

"How do you mean?"

"Just let it alone," Alice said. "It's been such a nice day. Don't spoil it."

"No, it's all right," Kircher said. "It needs explaining. I bought the place when Drew's folks sold. What happened," he told Ernest, "was that, as time went on, machines got bigger. And so did farms. What used to be maybe four or five places turned into one. There got to be more houses than there were people. They couldn't all be kept up. And then folks got used to more conveniences. My Helen, she wanted a new place. She said we'd earned a little comfort—"

"Well, we *had*. You can't deny it!"

"So I built her the ranch-style house over on the highway. For a while I kept this place mowed around. But then the creek crossing got bad, and it was hard to get over to do it. And then the old barn burned —"

"Burned?" Drew interrupted him. "Why, I just came by it this morning with the tree. It's full of hay. The horses are in their stalls."

"Yes," Kircher said, "but I mean eventually it burned. And after a while the sprouts and animals and the weather took the place. Anyway, that's how it happened."

"Well, I feel better knowing," said Ernest. "I always kind of wondered."

A sense of sweet completion filled the room. Then the ladies cleared, and their voices could be heard from the kitchen. And Drew went upstairs to see if he could find on the door frame the pencil lines that had marked his growing. And George Aylward, with a banker's natural privacy about such things, walked about looking in drawers to be certain he hadn't left any papers or documents behind.

Ernest Pryor and Karl Kircher, the first man and the last one, stood at the window together, looking down across the small field.

"To tell the truth," Kircher said, "I never really much cared to move. But I guessed I owed it to her. I'll say this, though. While I did live here, I took care of the place real good."

"It's all right," Ernest said. "It don't matter now."

"I used to come back, sometimes, to pick blackberries at the bottom of the field."

"Yes, that always was a good patch. Big berries."

"In fact, that's where I was when it happened. A queer kind of feeling came over me, so I sat down against a tree with my berry pail beside me. And for a minute I was afraid. But it turned out to be the easiest thing to do."

"They buried me on the place here," Ernest told him, "in that grove of big white oaks where the creek corners. Where'd they put you?"

Karl turned from the window with a surprised look.

"You know," he said, "I never thought to ask. It didn't seem important at the time."

*   *   *   *

The afternoon shadows of the trees beside the creek fell long across the snow. The young man worked his way slowly along the line, stopping and stooping where the muskrats had cut their runs just under the lip of the bank. The dozen sets all were empty as they'd been the day before. But he didn't mind. He wasn't serious about it, anyway. It was just a reason to be outdoors.

Neither did he mind leaving the game on TV before it ended, or the people before the day was quite finished. Christmas came every year. The faces at the table never changed, except to get a little older. The same stories, if you missed them, would come around again. He was still at that lucky age where it was not necessary yet to think very much about time.

He climbed through the snow, then, up to the house in its tangle of undergrowth. He wondered what kind of mess the drifters had left behind. There was no sign of them he could see. But they'd been there, he knew. He'd seen their light, and smelled their smoke — no doubt of that. And the broken iron stove, when he put his hand on it, still was warm to the touch.

He went back outside. Maybe the creek was trapped out, he thought. He could find another place, or he might just give it up. But he would remember the jungle of blackberry canes he'd found at the bottom of the field. It pleased him to think he might be the first one who'd discovered it. He would come back in the summer, when the berries were fat and sweet.

From December to July seemed to him like an eternity, almost. But looked at another way, it would be hardly any time at all.

Then he went down the field and stepped across the broken stone wall and went on with the unnoticed, unstoppable rush of his life.

The Man from the Agency

"**C**an you do forty minutes?" the administrator, Mrs. Rawlins, asked.

"Certainly," said the magician. "Or an hour, two hours. Whatever you like."

"An hour is too long. Their attention wanders, and they start to get out of hand. I'd say 30 or 40 minutes at the outside."

"Maybe I could just see how it goes."

"Fine. But 40 minutes will be plenty. What kind of stunts do you do?"

"*Stunts?*" he said.

"Yes, so I'll know what to expect."

"Well, I can do sleight-of-hand. Like this," he said, reaching across her desk to pluck a Kennedy half dollar from behind her ear.

"All right."

"Or this." He took a blue scarf from his pocket, fluttered it before her face, then wadded it in his fist. When he unfolded his hand, the scarf was gone.

"Yes, that's fine."

"You might look in your desk drawer," he told her.

The blue scarf was there.

"But those are just parlor tricks," he said. "Anyone can learn them. The rest is more interesting."

"And what, may I ask, is *the rest?*"

"That's a good deal harder to explain," said the magician. "Now, if I could see the venue."

"The what?"

"The room, if you don't mind."

His manner irritated her. From youngsters she expected evasiveness, but from adults she liked straight talk. She also was disappointed in his age. Children, in her experience, related best to someone younger. It hadn't occurred to her to ask the agency about that. Now he was here — looking less like a magician than like some pensioner come from a checkers game, with a halo of white hair and eye-glasses hanging against his sweater front from a cord around his neck. And it was too late to make a change. In the future she would be more explicit.

"Last year we had a Santa," she told him as they marched together down the hall.

"Did you?"

"It didn't work out," said Mrs. Rawlins. "In fact, it was a disaster. He smelled of drink."

"They often do."

"He got sick." Her voice rose thinly at the memory of it. "Here's the room."

It was plain as a handball court. Cut-outs of a sleigh and reindeer had been tacked high on one gray wall, and four long tables were set with paper plates, napkins, cups and plastic forks. On one side were three windows behind protective inner guards of heavy carpenter's screen. Snowflakes were taped to the screens. In all, the effect was institutional and sad.

"Good," the magician told Mrs. Rawlings. "This should do."

"We'll serve the refreshments first. You'll have your forty minutes. Then the staff will take over. How shall I introduce you?"

"It's not necessary. I'll simply begin."

"Will you need a place to get in costume?"

"No," he said. He wasn't carrying any satchel. "I'm dressed."

"All right. But please remember that some of our children are quite severely disturbed. And some have other problems. We try not to excite them."

He was looking around the room and hardly seemed to be listening. Mrs. Rawlins hoped he understood.

"Do we pay you directly," she asked, "or make it to the agency?"

"Yes," he told her. "This room will be fine."

*   *   *   *

"First," said the magician, "it's much too bright in here to do magic. Don't you agree?"

One or two of them nodded. Most were talking or quarreling, elbowing table mates, poking forks through their paper plates or otherwise occupied. He didn't own them yet. Children give themselves up cautiously, often with good reason.

"Magic is something that happens kind of in the corner of your eye," the magician said. "It can't stand too much light. So let's see what we can do about that."

He looked directly at the smallest girl at the near table.

"You are...?"

"Gloria," she answered, in a voice even smaller than herself.

"I *thought* so! It's a glorious name. Would you close the window curtains for me, Gloria?"

"There aren't any."

"Of course there are. Just pull them closed tight, if you will."

She did, and the room dimmed.

"And now, about these walls." He balanced his glasses on his nose and looked around in slow disapproval. "These walls need attention." He let his glasses fall down on the end of their cord.

"You!"

The magician's quick eyes skewered a heavy boy whose fist was drawn back to deliver a punch on the arm of the lad next to him.

"Yes, you — please! On this question of the walls."

"What about them," the boy said sullenly, hating to be singled out.

"They are puke-gray, these walls." That brought a ripple of laughter. None of them had ever heard a grown-up use the word.

"It's what color they've always been."

"Then we'll change it. We'll make a revolution, right here and now. What would you like to see up on that wall?"

The question was strange to the boy, who was unused to being asked what he liked. He had to think.

"A monkey," he said finally. "A bunch of monkeys."

The girl across from him made a disgusted sound with her lips.

"Monkeys are gross! Put something nice up there. Put up a sky with clouds. And some trees."

"Put birds in the trees."

"And a lotta flowers growing," said a voice from the far end of the room.

"Listen to Louie! He wants walls he can smell."

"Hey, we can smell you, Louie!"

"He can't see hardly anything," the small girl told the magician. "And he wets himself sometimes."

The old man waited for the racket to subside, then he began to pivot slowly, eyes fixed on the flat gray of the walls.

He saw a sky wider than any ocean, with clouds like islands floating in it. And in the great green forest under that sky, in trees of a kind only found in books, bright parrots fluttered, and hornbills with their enormous comical beaks. Troops of monkeys swung through the branches, picking leaves and fruit. And on the ground below, flowers were everywhere.

"I *can* see it," said Louie from the back.

They all could see it. He had them now.

"All right," said the magician, giving a last look at the walls to be sure they were satisfactory. "We've made us a good place to live. A place to be happy in. And now..."

He looked from one face to the next, all of them in turn — each of the more than 30 small faces at the tables. His eyes were so strange and bright they almost wanted to look away, but not one did.

"Now we're going to try something harder," he said. "I'm going to ask you to think of what you want most in the world. If you could have anything, what would it be?"

"*Anything?*" It was an incredulous whisper.

"Absolutely," the magician said.

"Does it have to be a thing?"

"No, there aren't any rules. No limits. Just whatever you want most. I don't know what that is. You do. But magic's always hard to work, and this piece is the hardest. We have to think about it together. Are you ready?"

He ran a hand through his fluff of hair. Then he frowned and pressed his fingers over both eyes in terrific concentration.

The room got as silent as a held breath.

*   *   *   *

The kitchen crew was finished tidying up, and some of them had come out to stand against the wall at the far end. The nurse was there, too. And several of the teachers.

Mrs. Rawlins stayed in the kitchen, her papers spread out on a borrowed table, writing names on the next day's work schedule.

"It's too quiet," she said. "What's going on out there."

"I don't know," said one of the servers. "They're all just sitting there. I think he's got them making up their imaginary wish lists."

"That's cruel. It's a wicked thing to do."

Her instinct had been right. The old man was trouble — as much trouble as a potted Santa. And he'd already run way over his time. Well, she could put an end to it. And she would have, except that when she came through the door, he looked at her with his finger to his lips, and she found she couldn't speak.

The children, the teachers, all of them — even Mrs. Rawlins herself, then — were quiet and motionless as sleepers. The only sound was the wind pushing the clouds across the walls, the rustle of the monkeys moving among the branches and the occasional croak of a bird.

And at the front of the room a wonderful and alarming thing was happening.

The old magician had begun taking on the shapes of other people, all ages and sizes and colors of them. Boys and girls, men and women, old people and even little babies — dissolving from one to another so fast it was hard to tell where they began and ended.

And the room filled with a sudden, enormous crowd that the magician had made.

Every child there felt the touch of a caring hand and the near presence of someone loved. And not only the children. It happened also to the teachers and cooks and the nurse and even Mrs. Rawlins. No one was alone. No one was left out. Each one was joined by a friend, or by a parent, even if that parent was far off, or a sweetheart or the child always wanted. Each one had the gift of someone to love and be loved by.

It lasted only a few moments, but they all were affected in a way they would never forget.

Then it passed, and the room brightened and the walls faded back to gray, with only the lingering suggestion of one cloud that might actually have been an old smudge.

"Well!" said Mrs. Rawlins to the magician, who had mostly resolved back into an old man again, and who looked rather tired.

"It's a nice trick." She had to compose herself to say it.

"Thanks. But that one's not a trick."

"Illusion, then."

"Whatever," said the magician and started away down the hall.

"Just a minute," she called after him.

He stopped with his hand on the street door, changing shapes just the least bit.

"What about the check?"

"Send it to the agency," he said. And then, as if by magic, he was gone.